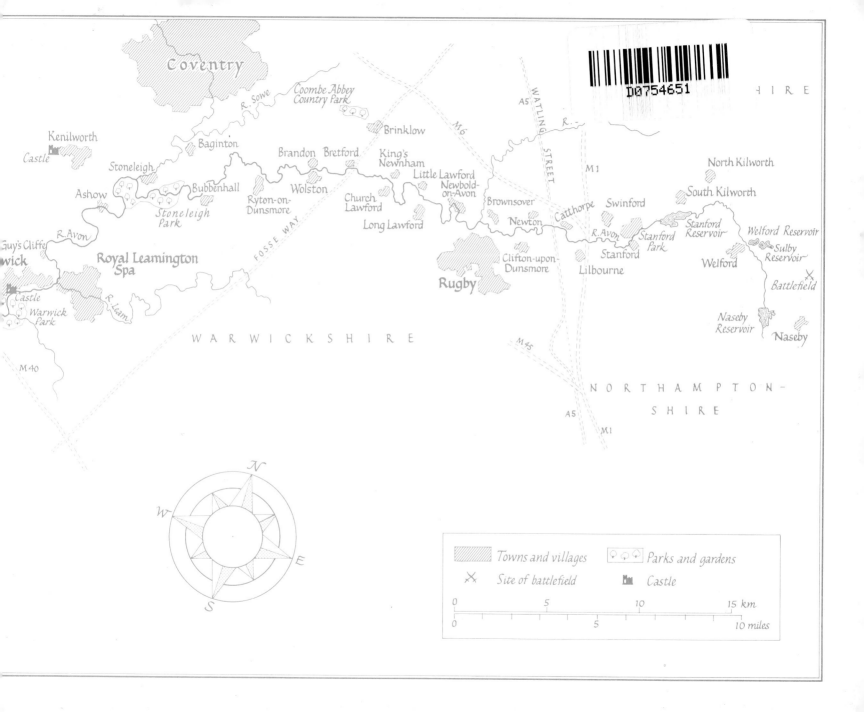

SHAKESPEARE'S — AVON —

A Journey from Source to Severn

PHOTOGRAPHS BY ROB TALBOT
TEXT BY ROBIN WHITEMAN

VIKING

VIKING

Published by the Penguin Group
27 Wrights Lane, London W8 5TZ, England
Viking Penguin Inc., 40 West 23rd Street, New York, New York 10010, USA
Penguin Books Australia Ltd, Ringwood, Victoria, Australia
Penguin Books Canada Ltd, 2801 John Street, Markham, Ontario, Canada L3R 1B4
Penguin Books (NZ) Ltd, 182–190 Wairau Road, Auckland 10, New Zealand

Penguin Books Ltd, Registered Offices: Harmondsworth, Middlesex, England

First published 1989

Colour origination by Colorlito, Milan
Typeset in 11/14pt Bembo (Linotron 202) by
Wyvern Typesetting Ltd, Bristol
Printed in Great Britain by
Butler & Tanner Ltd, Frome and London

A CIP catalogue record for this book is available from the British Library

ISBN 0-670-824968
LCCN 88-51907

Frontispiece: Anne Hathaway's Cottage

CONTENTS

Acknowledgements 6

Introduction 7

1 *NASEBY* 9 · *Naseby to Rugby* 14

2 *RUGBY* 23 · *Rugby to Coventry* 28

3 *COVENTRY* 39 · *Coventry to Kenilworth* 44

4 *KENILWORTH* 53 · *Kenilworth to Royal Leamington Spa* 58

5 *ROYAL LEAMINGTON SPA* 67 · *Royal Leamington Spa to Warwick* 72

6 *WARWICK* 75 · *Warwick to Stratford-upon-Avon* 82

7 *STRATFORD-UPON-AVON* 97 · *Stratford-upon-Avon to Evesham* 106

8 *EVESHAM* 121 · *Evesham to Pershore* 126

9 *PERSHORE* 135 · *Pershore to Tewkesbury* 140

10 *TEWKESBURY* 151

Photographic Notes 156

Properties Open to the Public 157

Tourist Information Offices and Other Useful Addresses 158

Select Bibliography 159

Index 160

ACKNOWLEDGEMENTS

Robin Whiteman and Rob Talbot would like to thank everyone who gave their time to guide them around the properties and sites featured in this book. They particularly wish to acknowledge the generous cooperation they received from The National Trust (Severn Region), The Shakespeare Birthplace Trust, Warwick Castle and The Warwickshire Nature Conservation Trust in allowing them unrestricted access to their properties and sites.

They are also grateful to: Lady Braye (Stanford Hall); Lord and Lady Leigh (Stoneleigh Abbey); Captain E.H. Lee, RN, and the Governors of Lord Leycester Hospital (Warwick); N.W.R. Mellon, Headmaster of King Edward VI Grammar School (Stratford-upon-Avon); Dr Peter Roberts (Warwickshire County Council); Nicola Russell (Royal Shakespeare Theatre); P.F. Latham, Town Clerk of Stratford-upon-Avon Town Council; Vale of Evesham Historical Society (Almonry Museum, Evesham); The Warwickshire Constabulary at Stratford-upon-Avon; the Rector and Churchwardens of the Collegiate Church of Holy Trinity (Stratford-upon-Avon); the Rector and Churchwardens of the Collegiate Church of St Mary the Virgin (Warwick); Joe Taylor, Senior Ranger, Coombe Abbey Country Park; John Beddington, miller of Charlecote Mill; Charlecote Nurseries; Snitterfield Fruit Farm; Miss Chapman (The Manor House, Naseby); Colin Potter and Roger Smith (WARNACT); Ann Wood (Barford); Henry Baker (Church Lawford).

Many individuals were of tremendous help, notably: for The National Trust – Michael and Annette Pickard (Charlecote Park); for the Shakespeare Birthplace Trust – Mrs Parsons (New Place), Malcolm Armsden (Hall's Croft), George Rooke (Birthplace), Mrs Green (Mary Arden's House), Charles Wilson and Ted Clark (Anne Hathaway's Cottage) and Shirley Watkins (Administrative Headquarters); for Warwick Castle – Martin Westwood (General Manager); for The Warwickshire Nature Conservation Trust – Dr J.W. Lewis (Conservation Officer).

Special thanks to: Dr Levi Fox, Director of The Shakespeare Birthplace Trust, and Miss Barbara Morley, Regional Information Officer, The National Trust (Severn Region); appreciation goes also to all those individuals and institutions too numerous to mention by name.

INTRODUCTION

Shakespeare's Avon meanders slowly through the heart of the English countryside, flowing through lush green meadows shaded by tall trees and weeping willows, past tranquil villages, ancient towns, historic castles, fruit-laden orchards, dappled woodland, stately mansions and deer-filled parks. This gentle river, with its wealth of historical, romantic and literary associations, passes through what Henry James described as 'the core and centre of the English world: midmost England, unmitigated England'.

It flows in a generally south-westerly direction for nearly a hundred miles through five counties. Paradoxically, for such a peaceful river, it begins and ends on the sites of two historic battles, Naseby and Tewkesbury, which determined the destiny of England for years afterwards.

According to Thorne, the nineteenth-century diarist, the Avon's 'interest arises mainly from its associations, but in them it is alone among English rivers – perhaps among the rivers of the world. What scenes and men are before us! Naseby, Evesham, Tewkesbury, Stratford: Wiclif, Shakespeare, Butler. Places among the most celebrated in our history, and each, in the events connected with it, productive of large results. Men each among the notablest of his age and country – each embodying and giving expression to its thought – one the notablest of any age, and destined to shape the thoughts of men through many ages.'

The man Thorne refers to as 'the notablest of any age' is, of course William Shakespeare. And it is with him, 'Sweet Swan of Avon' as Ben Jonson called him, that the river will always and pre-eminently be linked. Compared to rivers like the Amazon, Nile and Mississippi–Missouri, the Avon is small and insignificant. Yet the birth and death in Stratford-upon-Avon of this one man, and his subsequent international success as a poet and playwright, has impressed the name of this little river into the consciousness of the entire civilized world.

CHAPTER 1

NASEBY

The first major engagement of the English Civil War took place on 23 October 1642, at Edge Hill, ten miles to the east of Stratford-upon-Avon. It ended with an estimated 1,500 dead and both sides claiming victory.

According to the contemporary pamphlet *A Great Wonder in Heaven*, two months later, on Christmas Eve, a ghostly army re-enacted this bloody battle before the eyes of terrified 'shepherds and other countrymen, together with certain wayfarers'. At midnight could be heard 'first the sound of drums afar off and the noises of soldiers, as it were, giving out their last groans'. The sounds grew louder and closer, until the invisible battle raged all around them. Then, suddenly, there appeared out of the air the phantom armies of King Charles I and Parliament. The conflict continued for almost three hours – drums beating, cannon roaring, banners waving, horses neighing in terror and men screaming and shouting.

News of this supernatural event reached the king, who sent a number of his officers to investigate. It seems that a few weeks later they too witnessed the ghostly re-enactment, recognizing many of the men who had been killed. The story was confirmed under oath. At the time, it was considered to be an omen; but of what, no one knew.

Apparently, Charles I received a number of ghostly warnings during those troubled times. Three years after the battle of Edge Hill, he was at Daventry, Northamptonshire, with an army of around 9,000 men. That night, so the story goes, he was visited by the ghost of Thomas Wentworth, first Earl of

The village of Naseby and the parish church of All Saints

Thirteen miles north of Northampton, Naseby is close to the borders of Warwickshire and Leicestershire. It is a remote upland village, 623 feet above sea-level, situated on the great belt of limestone and clay that stretches from the coast of Dorset north-east through the Cotswolds to the coast of Yorkshire.

Strafford, who had been beheaded on his orders. The ghost told him 'that if he kept his resolution of fighting he was undone'. The apparition reappeared the following night to reinforce the warning.

Whatever the truth behind the story, the fact is that on 14 June 1645 the opposing armies met in a field near the village of Naseby. The Parliamentarian forces were under the command of Sir Thomas Fairfax, with Oliver Cromwell as lieutenant-general commanding the right flank. The Royalist forces were under the king, with Prince Rupert in actual command.

The Royalists were up against a superbly disciplined fighting force. The Parliamentarians had been trained to attack, re-form and attack again; the king's army had no such advantage. After the first charge, the king lost control of his forces and, inevitably, it lost him the battle. He fled the field leaving 'Fairfax master of all his foot, cannon, and baggage; amongst which was his own cabinet, where his most secret papers were, and letters between the queen and him' (Mastin). The letters contained evidence of the king's secret negotiations with foreign courts and were published by the authority of Parliament.

The tide turned against Charles and, four years later, he was executed. Parliament ruled the country and Cromwell rose from lieutenant-general to be Lord Protector of the Commonwealth.

In 1645 the battlefield to the north of Naseby village was open, with very few natural features, the most notable being a bank of trees to the west known as Sulby Hedge. The ground, however, was rough and uneven. As Joshua Sprigge, chaplain to General Fairfax, wrote in *Anglia Rediviva, England's Recovery* (1647), a rare eyewitness account of the battle:

Upon the enemy's approach, the Parliament's army marched up to the brow of the hill . . . In the meantime, the rest of the divisions of the right wing, being straightened by furzes on the right hand, advanced with great difficulty, as also by reason of the unevenness of the ground and a coney warren, over which they were to march, which put them somewhat out of their order in their advance.

The soil around Naseby is mainly red liassic clay and boulder clay, good for crops and even better for grazing. Naseby has only comparatively recently ceased to be a farming community, the majority of the inhabitants now working in the neighbouring towns.

Naseby's origins stretch back into antiquity. It has been suggested that it lies on the prehistoric Jurassic Way, the major route which ran across England from the Mendip Hills, in the south-west, to the Humber, in the north-east. It was originally called *Hnaefesburgh*, meaning 'the fortress of Hnaef'. Hnaef is an Old English personal name, which suggests that the settlement was early Saxon, probably dating from the sixth century AD. By 1086, according to the Domesday Book, *Hnaefesburgh* had become *Navesberie*, an Old English word

Legend tells that Cromwell was buried secretly in a field at Naseby, on the site of the Civil War battle of 1645 in which he was second-in-command to Fairfax. Although Cromwell's head ended up in the possession of his old college at Cambridge, Sidney Sussex, the fate of his body has never been conclusively resolved.

signifying 'a centre'. As late as the seventeenth century it was spelt *Navesby*.

In medieval times the village was granted a charter allowing it to hold a weekly market, and the shaft of the last market cross is situated near the parish church of All Saints.

Not surprisingly, the great battle of 1645 features prominently in Naseby's history. A number of relics have been unearthed from the battlefield over the centuries, including human bones, swords, stirrup irons, cannon and musket balls and even a button from an unknown soldier's tunic. Many of these items are housed in the Naseby Battle and Farm Museum, where there is also a model of the battle. Two monuments commemorate that decisive day in June, 1645: an obelisk erected in 1823 and a more recent memorial with a ball on top, which

is on the site of the battle.

In 1820, when the Enclosure Act affecting Naseby was passed by Parliament, the open-field system was abolished in favour of small fields separated by hedgerows. Within three years the landscape had changed irreversibly. As the Revd John Mastin had remarked some thirty years earlier:

no field in Northamptonshire would answer better by inclosure, than that of Naseby. Here is good strong land; fine glades for meadows; red hills, good for turnips and artificial grasses, black woodcock, or falling land, now grass, but much improved by ploughing. Some few bogs, which might either by under-draining be laid dry, or rendered still more valuable by being planted.

'Naseby is a delightful summer residence, presenting to the eye almost unbounded prospects,' he added, clearly with the intention of attracting visitors to the village. 'It is no exaggeration to say, that thirty-nine, or forty parish churches may be seen by the naked eye from one station, an old windmill bank in Naseby field.'

Inside the parish church of All Saints, the earliest part of which dates from the thirteenth century, is 'Cromwell's Table' at which, reputedly, a group of Royalist soldiers were eating and drinking on the eve of the battle when they were captured by a party of Parliamentarian scouts.

In the fifteenth century the church spire was left by the builders as a truncated stump. It remained uncompleted until the eighteenth century when a large copper ball, topped by a weather vane, was added. According to Mastin, the hollow ball, rumoured to be able to hold 60 gallons of ale, was originally brought from Boulogne in 1544 by Sir Gyles Allington of Horseheath, Cambridgeshire. When the church was restored in 1859–60 the huge ball was removed and it is now in the churchyard.

One of the many springs in and around Naseby rises near the church and, after receiving other waters, becomes a river. It is here at Naseby, near the field of battle, that Shakespeare's Avon begins.

NASEBY TO RUGBY

The 'official' source of the River Avon is in the garden of the Manor House, Naseby, opposite the church of All Saints. The spot, 600 feet above sea-level, is marked by a tall cast-iron cone, standing under a large chestnut tree and hidden from the road by a brick wall. It is reported that at one time the water from the spring ran up the centre of the cone, poured out of the receptacles at the top and dropped into the sunken stone-lined basin below. On the side of the cone there are the words 'Source of the Avon 1822'. Now, although the spring seems to have shifted a few yards, to emerge from the nearby garden path, the basin at the foot of the cone still contains water.

From the grounds of the Manor House, the infant Avon flows under the wall and beneath Newlands road to emerge in a well in the garden of the Fitzgerald Arms. The water can be traced in the cellar of the old inn, where it bubbles up through the stone flags of the floor, only to disappear just as rapidly.

It next appears in the open fields to the west of the village, trickling through culverts and running through ditches before entering Naseby Reservoir. In 1820, when the fields around Naseby were enclosed, sixty-two acres were awarded to the Grand Union Canal Company for access to the reservoir. The Grand Union Canal runs from the River Thames, at Brentford, to Birmingham, with several branches leading elsewhere. Naseby Reservoir is used not only to help fill the Grand Union Canal, but also for fishing and sailing.

'For a few miles farther there is nothing of interest along our river,' wrote Thorne in 1845, adding,

It runs along wide fields, somewhile hidden by the tangled bramble-bushes, and presently careering in broad daylight. It will lead us, if we follow it, through many a little quiet, thoroughly secluded, nook, past homely cottages, with their picturesque tenantry; by solitary farm-houses, reminding us, by their plain substantial working-day air, of olden times; and among a people fresher and less sophisticated than by our great roads . . . there are quiet little groups of houses . . . tame all as the cattle that wander about the closes.

The landscape has changed little since Thorne's description. Rolling hills with lush meadows, green pastures and rich arable land are divided by long

The source of the Avon at Naseby

The 'official' source of the river is in the grounds of the old Manor House. Because of the numerous springs hereabouts the exact source is impossible to determine. Thorne sites the source, 'Avon Well', in the garden of 'the little inn opposite Naseby church'. He notes that the water used to spout from the bill of a plaster swan until it was used as a target by stone-throwing locals.

The infant Avon running through fields west of Naseby
The exact source of the Avon is difficult to trace and the waters that flow west from the village are swallowed by the Naseby Reservoir. A little stream emerges from the northern end of the reservoir and here, without doubt, the infant Avon begins its slow winding journey to the Severn.

hedgerows and the occasional wooded copse. It is overwhelmingly rural and entirely English in character with isolated farms, old manor-houses, small cottages and soaring church spires.

The infant Avon winds from Naseby Reservoir through reed-flanked meadows to Naseby Hall, where it forms a small lake. This is the country of the Pytchley Hunt, founded by the first Earl Spencer in 1761.

About a mile north of the Hall the river passes the

remains of Sulby Abbey, a convent founded in the twelfth century by William de Wydeville, or Wyvile, Lord of Welford. 'It is now a respectable farm house,' wrote Ireland in 1795, 'and has only a few fragments of old stone walls, decorated with heads of monks, &c. here and there scattered about, to indicate what was its original destination.' Various fragments from the time of the abbey have been incorporated into the farm buildings.

The Avon turns north-westwards near the site of the abbey and, passing the adjoining reservoirs of Sulby and Welford, is crossed by the first of many road bridges. The bridge at Welford is in fact two small bridges joined together: one spanning the Avon and the other the feeder to the Welford arm of the Grand Union Canal. The castellated Wharf House Inn straddles the borders of Northampton-shire and Leicestershire. Encroached upon by thick reeds, the river brushes the south side of the inn, while the Welford arm of the canal terminates on the north, where there are moorings for holiday craft.

Welford (not Welford-on-Avon, which is beyond Stratford-upon-Avon) is a village built mainly of brick, with a stone-built manor-house.

The canal and the Avon run alongside each other for just over a mile before they separate near Bosworth Mill Farm, where the canal joins the Leicester branch of the Grand Union Canal. The river turns south-westwards to North Kilworth

The Avon near Welford
Many of the small streams that contribute to the River Avon were straightened and channelled into 'drains' when the surrounding fields were enclosed during the early nineteenth century.

Mill Farm. The building housing the farm's water-wheel was demolished in 1947 and the farm and stables stand empty and derelict; the mill lies at the end of a long bridleway.

Just beyond South Kilworth the river has been dammed to form Stanford Reservoir which supplies the Rugby area. After emerging from the reservoir, it enters the wooded parkland of Stanford Hall, where it has been widened to create a seemingly navigable stream before it flows into a lake.

STANFORD HALL

Stanford Hall was built by the Smiths of Warwick for Sir Roger Cave at the end of the seventeenth century, when the old manor-house was pulled down. It has been the historic seat of the Cave family for over five hundred years. Lady Braye, the eighth baroness and current owner, is directly descended from Peter Cave, brother of the vicar of Stanford and nephew of the abbot of Selby, who first came to live at Stanford in 1430.

The Hall stands on the Leicestershire bank of the Avon, while the church and the village of Stanford-on-Avon stand on the opposite bank in Northamptonshire.

The parish of Stanford is ancient. It is mentioned in the Domesday Book of 1086 and shortly afterwards it was granted to the Benedictine abbey of Selby in Yorkshire by the Norman, Wide de Reinbuedcurt. The historic document of 1140, in which King Stephen made a further grant of Stanford land to the abbey, is preserved in the library of the Hall. After the Dissolution of the Monasteries, Sir Thomas Cave bought the manor from the Crown in 1540.

The Norman church at Stanford-on-Avon was built on the site of a Saxon church and much of the present building dates from 1307. It is noted for its well-preserved monuments of the Cave family and for its beautiful stained-glass windows, parts of which date from the reign of Edward II.

The seventeenth-century organ, according to Ireland, 'formerly belonged to the banquetting room at Whitehall, which, by order of Cromwell, was taken down and sold. It was intended to be placed in

The derelict buildings of North Kilworth Mill Farm The Avon is now a narrow stream, often choked with reeds, meandering through lonely pastures where meadowsweet and thistles, dog roses and nettles mingle in the tangled hedgerows. The stream runs slowly through the farm meadows, its original course through the mill-race now overgrown with dense rushes.

the chapel of Magdalen College, Oxford, but being too small, was purchased by the Cave family for this church.' Apparently, it was brought from Oxford by barge on the Grand Union Canal.

Stanford Hall contains many historical items, including antique furniture, paintings, tapestries and costumes. In the library, stocked with about 5,000 books, papers and documents, there are some relics once thought to have come from the battle of Naseby. The stable block now houses the Pilcher Aviation Museum and across the river is a monument to Lieutenant Percy Pilcher, RN, 'the first man to fly in England'. It was erected by the Royal Aeronautical Society of Great Britain and marks the spot where he was killed in 1899 during an exhibition flight in which he crashed.

Stanford Hall

The house and grounds are open to the public on certain days from Easter to the end of September. There are also many special one-day events, including car and motor-cycle rallies, hot-air balloon meetings, hovercraft races, gundog training rallies and raft races. The historic collection of vehicles in the Motor-cycle and Car Museum are all in running order and many are used for rallies.

In Ireland's opinion Stanford park's 'greatest ornament is the beautiful sheet of water that is formed by our Avon, and which runs at a very proper distance from the mansion'. The river, frequented by moorhens, coots, mute swans and great crested grebes, contains a variety of fish, including perch, dace, carp and pike. As it leaves the park it becomes, once again, a small stream meandering through green fields and willow-hung water-meadows.

Swinford, situated on the opposite side of the

Avon to Stanford-on-Avon, is an ancient village. It is mentioned in the Domesday Book and there is some evidence that the de Swineford family may have held possessions in the area. In 1216, however, the Lord of the Manor was Hugh Revell, whose family ceased to have any further associations with Swinford in the fourteenth century. The Revells were followed by many other families whose interest in the lordship was transitory. In 1780, when an Act was passed for the enclosure of about 1,400 acres of Swinford land, the Lord of the Manor was Sir Thomas Cave of nearby Stanford Hall.

Flowing beneath the motorway, the Avon passes through rich pastureland and heads towards Lilbourne.

On the opposite bank is Catthorpe, a village surrounded by busy main roads. John Dyer, the poet, who became vicar of Catthorpe in 1741, lived in the parsonage near the church. He was the author of *Grongar Hill* and *The Fleece*: the latter work prompted Wordsworth to call him 'Bard of the Fleece' in his sonnet *To the Poet, John Dyer*.

To the west of the village, the Avon passes through the ancient arches of Dow, or Dove, Bridge and under the single-arched span carrying Watling Street, into the county of Warwickshire.

The skyline to the south of the river is now dominated by a vast network of aerials belonging to Rugby Radio Station, which was opened in 1926. It was once one of the world's largest radio transmitting stations, but it is now being overtaken by satellite communication.

After Dow Bridge the Avon threads its way towards Rugby under disused railway embankments, main roads and even canals. About a mile downstream from the bridge, on a small hill, stands the village of Clifton-upon-Dunsmore with its thirteenth-century church of St Mary. The name of the village is derived from the Saxon word *Clive*, meaning 'a rocky place' and also 'shelving ground'.

On the opposite side of the river is Newton, a small village which partly belonged to the Priory of Kenilworth until the Dissolution. Although the village is about half a mile from the Avon, the manor-house is sited close to the river on its twisting north bank.

The Castle Mounds at Lilbourne
These grassy mounds are now thought to have been a Norman motte and bailey. They were once said to be Tripontium, *the Roman encampment mentioned in the* Itinerary of the Emperor Antonine *(c. third century AD), but the site of* Tripontium *has been identified as being a few miles farther north-west, near Churchover.*

At Brownsover an aqueduct carries the waters of the Oxford Canal across the Avon. Brownsover, now a suburb of Rugby, was once a small village and, as the 'over' implies, it is situated on a hill. It is the traditional birthplace of Lawrence Sheriff, the founder of Rugby School, who is supposed to have been born here in about 1515. The timbered house is situated in Brownsover Lane, near Brownsover Hall Hotel. The Hall was built by Sir George Gilbert Scott, who also partly rebuilt the thirteenth-century church of St Michael in 1877.

Lutterworth, about six miles north of Browns-over, is the village where the religious reformer John Wyclif lived while he was translating the Latin Bible into English. He died on 31 December 1384, when, according to Ireland, 'he was struck with a paralysis while preaching at his parish church, and as his parishioners were conveying him from thence in a chair to his Rectory house, expired in his way thither'.

About forty years after his death, Wyclif's writings were condemned and the Council of Constance ordered that his body should be exhumed and burnt. His ashes were thrown into the Swift and, according to Wordsworth,

The Oxford Canal, near Clifton-upon-Dunsmore
The canal, seventy-eight miles long, runs from the River Thames at Oxford to Hawkesbury, north of Coventry, where it joins the Coventry Canal.

As thou these ashes, little Brook! wilt bear
Into the Avon, Avon to the tide
Of Severn, Severn to the narrow seas,

Into main Ocean they . . . shall spread, throughout the world dispersed.

CHAPTER 2
RUGBY

Rocheberie, as Rugby was called in the Domesday Book, is a Saxon name, thought to be derived from Hroca, a personal name, and 'bury', a hill fortress. It later became Rokebi, then Rokeby and, finally, Rugby.

The population of the village at the time of the Norman survey was probably less than one hundred. The village was situated on a plateau between the less populated Forest of Arden and the intensely cultivated Feldon, or 'field-land', in the south.

Today, the name of Rugby has acquired many different associations: to the scholar it means the public school; to the sportsman it means the game of Rugby football; to the builder it means Rugby Portland Cement; to the farmer and stock-breeder it means the cattle market; to the telecommunications expert it means the radio station; to the train enthusiast it is a major junction in the railway network; and to the local population it is a busy industrial town.

Rugby lies between the great Roman roads of Watling Street and the Fosse Way, which meet at High Cross some eight miles north of the town. The nearest Roman settlement was at *Tripontium*, on Watling Street, near the present-day village of Churchover.

After the Roman legions withdrew from Britain, early in the fifth century AD, the country was left undefended. The native Britons found themselves under attack not only from the Picts and Scots in the north, but also from overseas. The Avon valley was settled in the sixth century by both Angles and Saxons: the former coming from the east, to the upper Avon valley; the latter

Aerial view of Rugby

*View across the
Warwickshire countryside
towards Rugby*

from the south, to the middle and lower Avon valley. In time the area came to be divided between the kingdom of South Mercia, in the north and east, and the kingdom of the Hwicce, in the south-west. Within these two kingdoms there also existed smaller tribal territories. Eventually, Mercia absorbed the surrounding kingdoms, and became the largest and most important kingdom in Britain.

The height of Mercia's power was reached in the eighth century under Offa, who was responsible for constructing the massive earthwork dyke, evidence of which can still be found, along the Welsh border.

From the mid ninth century Mercia was under attack from the Danes, who by 868, according to the 'Anglo-Saxon Chronicle', had control of Nottingham. But Alfred, King of Wessex, defeated the Danes at the battle of Ethandun in 878 and established, by treaty, the limits of Danish territory. A line formed by the River Thames and Watling Street became the boundary between the territory known as 'Danelaw', to the north, and the English kingdoms of Mercia and Wessex, to the south.

Hostilities between the English and Danes were renewed after Alfred's death and several battles were fought in the Rugby area. The town, situated on high ground close to the border, was a fortified settlement of some strategic importance. There is evidence that it remained so until the mid twelfth century when Rugby Castle, probably a moated manor-house modified by King Stephen, was pulled down on the orders of Henry II.

The castle stood near the present-day Regent Place, a short distance north of the church of St Andrew. The oldest part of the church is the west tower, dating from the mid fourteenth century. There is a story that the fortified tower was built by Henry de Rokeby to get round the fact that Rugby was not allowed to have a castle – it is clearly defensive as well as ecclesiastical.

Not far from the church is Rugby School, founded by Lawrence Sheriff. Sheriff is said to have been born at Brownsover, a village two miles to the north of Rugby. He was apprenticed to a London grocer, William Walcott, and in 1541 he was admitted to the freedom of the Worshipful Company of Grocers. By 1551 he was supplying goods as 'purveyor by appointment' to Hatfield Palace, the home of the young Princess Elizabeth.

Throughout the short and bloody reign of Queen Mary he remained loyal to Princess Elizabeth and the Protestant cause. When Elizabeth succeeded to the throne in 1558 she rewarded many of her supporters, Sheriff among them. He prospered and used his wealth to buy property and land. In 1560, with his wife Elizabeth, he purchased a twenty-four-acre field called Conduit Close in Middlesex, half a mile north of the outskirts of London. It cost them £320. This piece of land was in later years to play a crucial role in the development of Rugby School.

In 1567 Sheriff became seriously ill and drew up his will. He left explicit instructions that 'his lands, tenements, and hereditaments in the county of Warwick', together with a sum of one hundred pounds, should be used by his trustees for the foundation of a 'school house and almshouses in Rugby'. The lands referred to were the rectory of Brownsover and the house in Rugby, which he had inherited from his father.

A 'fair and convenient school house' had to be added to the house in Rugby together with four almshouses. The house was to be the residence of the schoolmaster, who had to be 'an honest discrete and learned man, being a Master of Arts . . . to teach a Free Grammar School in the said school house'. The school was to be open chiefly 'to the children of Rugby and Brownsover aforesaid, and next for such as be of other places thereunto adjoining'.

Sheriff's illness did not prevent him from making a final journey to Rugby to arrange for the building of the school and almshouses. Before he returned to London he revoked the legacy of one hundred pounds and in its stead bequeathed one third part of Conduit Close, amounting to eight acres.

Why he should have changed his mind is a mystery. Conduit Close was at that time worth very little. But, as the centuries passed and the capital expanded, those few acres increased enormously in value, much to the benefit of Rugby School.

Lawrence Sheriff was buried in London on 16 September 1567. The school was founded shortly after and built in the same style as the King Edward VI Grammar School, Stratford-upon-Avon, though slightly smaller.* In the mid eighteenth century a new school was built and by 1783 the original schoolhouse had been demolished.

Rugby School became one of the foremost schools in the country under Dr Thomas Arnold, who was headmaster from 1828 to 1842. Life in the school under Dr Arnold is described in *Tom Brown's Schooldays*.

It was just prior to the period of Dr Arnold's headmastership that a boy named William Ellis, according to a plaque in the school, 'with a fine disregard

The quadrangle of Rugby School, renowned as the setting for Thomas Hughes's Tom Brown's Schooldays *and for its headmaster, Dr Thomas Arnold*

Founded in 1567 by Lawrence Sheriff, no part of the original school building remains. The Old Quadrangle was designed by Henry Hakewill in the early nineteenth century. William Butterfield was responsible for its western continuation and the distinctive octagonal tower of the chapel, built in 1872.

* Sheriff's loyalty to Queen Elizabeth I had been rewarded by the granting of a coat of arms and these arms were adopted by the school.

for the rules of football as played in his time, first took the ball in his arms and ran with it, thus originating the distinctive feature of the Rugby game, AD 1823'.

RUGBY TO COVENTRY

Among the famous men educated at Rugby School were Matthew Arnold (the eldest son of Dr Arnold), C.L. Dodgson (Lewis Carroll), William Temple (Archbishop of Canterbury), Rupert Brooke and Walter Savage Landor.

Landor wrote a number of poems recalling his childhood days in Warwickshire. In his *Last Fruit Off an Old Tree*, written when he was seventy-eight, he included a poem entitled 'On Swift Joining Avon near Rugby':

> *In youth how often at thy side I wander'd!*
> *What golden hours, hours numberless,*
> * were squander'd*
> *Among thy sedges, while sometimes*
> *I meditated native rhymes,*
> *And sometimes stumbled upon Latian feet.*

The course of the Avon, from its confluence with the Swift at Brownsover, takes it through the industrial complexes and housing estates of north Rugby. For nearly two miles it threads towards open countryside beyond Newbold-on-Avon.

Thorne called Newbold 'a strange odd place' and added,

There is about its meadows an absolute *plexus* of canals and railways, running under and over each other in a quite unaccountable manner: now beneath the road, now above it; under the church, across the river, in all directions, and sending out tentacula in a marvellous fashion. On the map they all look simple enough, but in reality are quite incomprehensible.

There are a number of disused watermills on this part of the Avon. The Avon Mill Inn, on the Newbold Road, probably stands on or near the site of the mill at Rugby mentioned in the Domesday Book. Part of the mill house was converted into an inn in the nineteenth century. The mill closed in 1930 and a car-park now occupies the site of the tail-race.

The mill at Long Lawford, of which no trace remains, was valued at fourteen shillings in the survey of 1086. From the late twelfth century it belonged to the monks of Pipewell Abbey, Northamptonshire. A fire destroyed both the fulling mill and the corn mill in 1328.

Little Lawford Mill was also held by Pipewell Abbey. It ceased production in the 1920s and is now

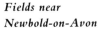

a farmhouse. The internal waterwheel has been removed but the mill stream still runs under the red-brick building and into the Avon at Little Lawford Ford.

From Newbold-on-Avon the river passes below the red-sandstone, hill-top church of St Botolph and loops through the valley to Little Lawford.

In the Domesday Book Little Lawford was recorded as *Lilleford*. Near the ford is a stone-built house with the date of 1604 above the porch. The building was originally part of Lawford Hall, demolished in about 1790.

On rising ground to the south of Little Lawford is the populous village of Long Lawford, divided in two by the Rugby-to-Coventry railway line. It was described in the Domesday Book as *Lellevort* or *Leileford*. The grey-brick church of St John was built in 1839 and is in the parish of Newbold-on-Avon, from which it is separated by the Avon and another railway line.

About half a mile downstream from Little Lawford the river passes the 'once celebrated Newnham Bath', described by Ireland as being 'famed for the cure of scorbutic and other disorders. It is said to have had great efficacy in closing and healing green wounds. It has a milky taste,' he continued, 'and issues from a mineral spring about a mile distant, from whence, passing a lime pit, it receives its chief salubrious quality.' In 1795 he observed that 'This well is still much frequented, and would probably be much more so, were the roads kept in a passable state.' Now, although the road is in good order, the baths have gone.

The Newnham Regis Baths were famous in the reign of Elizabeth I as a cure for gout, rheumatism and dyspepsia. In 1582 the Queen's physician, Dr Walter Bailey, published a paper proclaiming the great merits of the waters, but warns drinkers 'never to adventure to drink above six, or at the utmost eight pints in one day'.

From the site of the former baths, the Avon loops southwards through lush grazing meadows and rich farming land to double back on itself and resume its south-western course at King's Newnham.

King's Newnham, or Newnham Regis, stands on a low hill overlooking the valley and, as the name implies, once belonged to the Crown. The property was held by the monks of Kenilworth from the twelfth century until the Dissolution.

Three fish-ponds can be seen opposite the Georgian manor-house and in the farmyard there is a tall tower, partly covered by ivy. The structure is all that remains of the old church of St Lawrence, which was demolished towards the end of the eighteenth century. The original church was probably built by the monks in the thirteenth century.

In the vicinity of King's Newnham, particularly in the limestone pits, now disused, have been discovered the prehistoric remains of elephant, mammoth, rhinoceros, ox and, in 1822, the first hyena to be found in England.

Church Lawford lies on the south side of the Avon valley, opposite King's Newnham. It is an ancient village, mentioned in the survey of 1086, with a church that was rebuilt in 1872. The church of St Peter and the old Elizabethan manor-house nearby overlook fields through which the river flows.

In 1901, when Charles Showell published his

Shakespeare's Avon, Newnham Mill was a large, three-storey building with two waterwheels and probably dated from the mid nineteenth century. It closed around twenty years later and is now little more than a pile of overgrown rubble.

As the Avon heads westwards towards Coventry, through fields of rape and corn, it passes the villages of Bretford, Marston, Wolston and Brandon.

At Bretford the Roman Fosse Way once crossed the river by a 'broad ford', hence the village's name. Now, the river is spanned by a narrow bridge, only able to carry a single line of traffic. Just over a mile north of Bretford, the ancient road runs through Brinklow, where there are the remains of a castle, thought by some to pre-date the Romans. Others,

however, consider the earthworks to have been built in the twelfth century during the reign of King Stephen.

About a mile downstream from Bretford, where Geoffrey de Clinton founded a cell for nuns, is Marston or, as Dugdale calls it, Merston juxta Wolston. The mill, 'being situate flat and low near the River, where the soil is naturally marish' or marshy, was demolished many years ago but the miller's house is still occupied.

Below Marston, the Avon and the Rugby-to-Coventry railway line divide the two villages of Wolston and Brandon; the former is situated almost at river level and the latter on rising ground. At the beginning of this century Showell wrote:

Brandon has no church, but is a bright, clean, happy and prosperous-looking village, with a working-man's club and institute. Wolston is a large village, has a very fine, interesting old church, yet it is a cheerless, thriftless-looking place, where apparently nothing is done to brighten the lives of its people.

Both villages are mentioned in the Domesday Book. At *Brandune*, as Brandon was then known, there was a mill rated at twenty-six pence. In the twelfth century the Normans built a castle on the north bank of the Avon. It was pulled down in the following century during the Barons' War against

Farm buildings and the remains of the church at King's Newnham, with Church Lawford on the opposite side of the Avon valley
In 1854 Lord John Douglas-Scott excavated the foundations of the church and discovered several lead coffins, one of them containing the remains of the first Earl of Chichester, the great-grandson of Sir Thomas Leigh of Stoneleigh.

King Henry III. The remains can still be seen near the railway station, opposite the church of St Margaret, Wolston, or *Uluestone*.

To the east of Wolston there was a priory thought to have been founded shortly after the Conquest as a cell of St Peter's Convent at Dinan in France. This does not appear to have prospered, however, and in the late fourteenth century it was sold to 'the Prior and Convent of Carthusians near Coventry, then lately founded by King Richard II'.

The Avon between Wolston and Brandon
During the Ice Age the entire Avon valley, from the hills around Naseby to the Vale of Evesham, was one vast lake. Melting waters and countless glacial advances and retreats laid down deposits of sand, clay and gravel on the lake floor. Consequently, there are numerous quarries and gravel-pits along the valley. Many of the old flooded pits, as at Brandon Marsh, are now nature reserves.

South of the village, on Lammas Hill, is an ancient round barrow and beyond is the tract of high ground known as Dunsmore Heath. Although it is now mostly cultivated, this land was once the legendary haunt of the Dun Cow, the monstrous creature which was slain by Guy of Warwick (see p. 61).

From Brandon and Wolston the Avon, now broad enough to be called a river, flows through flat green meadows, bright with flowers in early spring. But gone, except on protected sites, are the flower-rich meadows and river banks so typical of the countryside described by Shakespeare in *Love's Labour's Lost*:

> *When daisies pied, and violets blue,*
> *And lady-smocks all silver white,*
> *And cuckoo-buds of yellow hue,*
> *Do paint the meadows with delight.*

The nature reserve at Brandon Marsh, managed by the Warwickshire Nature Conservation Trust (WARNACT), boasts a rich variety of plant, animal and insect life. It is considered to be the best site for both resident and migrant birds along the Avon valley.

The reserve contains many plants that were once widespread in the valley, including marsh mari-golds, yellow irises, primroses, meadowsweet and orchids. In season these flowers attract a host of insects, which in turn help to support the flourish-ing bird population.

The heron, or handsaw as Shakespeare referred to it, is often seen feeding along the banks of the Avon. At Coombe Abbey, two miles to the north of Brandon Marsh, is the largest heronry in Warwick-shire, containing over twenty breeding pairs. In 1972 the lake and its were designated a Site of Special Scientific Interest by the Nature Con-servancy Council.

Coombe Abbey: the west front, added by William Winde between 1680 and 1691

The abbey, now known as Coombe Abbey Country Park, is open to the public from dawn to dusk. Amongst the park's many attractions are an adventure playground, picnic areas, exhibitions, angling, boating and woodland walks. Throughout the year medieval banquets are staged in the moated house.

COOMBE ABBEY

The Cistercian abbey at Coombe was founded by Richard de Camville in 1150 and ratified by Robert, Earl of Leicester during the reign of Henry II. By the end of the thirteenth century, the abbey monks owned a large amount of property, including land at Little Lawford, Newton, Wolston, Churchover, Brinklow and nearby Binley.

In 1539, at the Dissolution, the abbey was partially demolished and the structures that remained were utilized for living accommodation. In 1581, the estate passed, by marriage, to Sir John Harington, who incorporated parts of the old mon-astery buildings into a two-storey house built partly of stone and partly of wood.

The Haringtons were kinsfolk of James VI of Scotland and when James succeeded Elizabeth I to the throne of England in 1603, Sir John was created first Baron Harington of Exton. The king entrusted the education and upbringing of his seven-year-old daughter, Princess Elizabeth, to Lord Harington. Coombe Abbey was her principal residence from 1603 to 1608, during which time the Gunpowder Plot conspirators made plans to kidnap her.

The plot to blow up the king and Parliament had been hatched by the local Catholic gentry and in November 1605 they assembled a large armed force on Dunsmore Heath, ostensibly for a hunt. In reality they were awaiting the news from London that Guy Fawkes and his accomplices had succeeded in their task, whereupon they were to ride upon Coombe, seize the princess and make her queen. Harington, however, heard of the conspiracy and took Elizabeth to Coventry until the danger had passed. In the event, the plot failed. Guy Fawkes was caught and his supporters, who fled in panic, were either captured or killed. Elizabeth later married Frederick V, the Elector Palatine, and was briefly the 'Winter Queen' of Bohemia.

From 1622 until 1923, the Coombe Abbey estate belonged to the Craven family. They added a new west front, designed by William Winde, between 1680 and 1691. The grounds and surrounding parkland were landscaped by Lancelot 'Capability' Brown in about 1771. The estate was acquired by Coventry Corporation between 1953 and 1964 and is now known as Coombe Abbey Country Park.

———————

About a mile below Brandon, according to Ireland in 1795, there was a mill 'employed in making a coarse brown paper for the use of hot presses'. It was converted to silk spinning in the 1820s, but when Showell passed it at the beginning of the twentieth century it had become 'a large silk mill out of repair'. Today only the foundations remain.

A short distance downstream from the ruins of Brandon Mill is the hill-top village of Ryton-on-Dunsmore, at the western extremity of Dunsmore Heath. There was a mill and a church at Ryton in 1086; little is left of the mill, but the red and grey sandstone church of St Leonard, restored in 1887 and again in 1891, dates from before 1100 and exhibits early Norman and early English work.

During the Second World War an aircraft shadow factory, which has now become a massive industrial complex for the production of motor vehicles, was erected to the west of Ryton-on-Dunsmore.

North of the giant Ryton automobile works, the Avon flows through flat marshland, a large reed-filled stretch of water frequented by reed warblers, coots and moorhens.

Beyond the marsh the Avon passes through the long tunnel of Ryton Bridge. Since Ireland,

Thorne, Showell and Quiller-Couch journeyed down the Avon the bridge has undergone considerable widening, with two further bridges now attached to the original structure. From here the busy London road heads towards the spires of Coventry, three miles to the north-west.

CHAPTER 3
COVENTRY

In 1642, Nehemiah Wharton (quoted by Poole) described Coventry as 'a city environed with a wall, coequal, if not exceeding that of London, for breadth and height; and with gates and battlements, magnificent churches and stately streets, and abundant fountains of water; altogether a place very sweetly situate'.

It has been argued that the name 'Coventry' is derived from 'convent town', since a convent or nunnery was founded here in the seventh century 'by the Holy Virgin St Osburg'. The site was on high ground in the Forest of Arden where a spring, thought to be sacred, bubbled out of the ground. The convent prospered and a small community grew up around it. The settlement over-looked the River Sherbourne which, via the River Sowe, enters the Avon at Stoneleigh. However, the more widely accepted explanation for the city's name is that Coventry means 'Cofa's tree' and is derived from *Cofa*, a personal name, and the Anglo-Saxon *treo*, meaning 'a tree'.

The convent was destroyed by the Danes in the year 1016. Twenty-seven years later Leofric, Earl of Mercia and husband of Lady Godiva, founded a Benedictine monastery on the site. His gift was confirmed by a charter granted by Edward the Confessor.

A woman of piety and a patron of several religious institutions, Lady Godiva is said to have begged her husband to lower the taxes he had imposed on the people of the town. At first he refused to listen to her but finally, out of exasperation, he said,

Coventry Cathedral,
Coventry

Lady Godiva's statue, Broadgate, Coventry
After riding naked through the town, Godiva 'returned rejoicing to her husband', who freed 'the City of Coventry from its servitude'. Godiva became a symbol of civic freedom and in Coventry her famous ride was celebrated by an annual procession until the end of the nineteenth century and periodically thereafter. In a niche above one of the precincts is a painted effigy of Peeping Tom.

'Mount your horse naked, and ride through the market of the town from beginning to end when all the people are assembled, and when you return you shall have your wish.'

Godiva replied, 'And if I am willing to act thus, will you grant me leave?'

And Leofric said, 'I will.'

Godiva sent word to the inhabitants that they should stay indoors and refrain from looking out of their windows. She then removed her clothes, mounted her white horse, let down her hair to cover her nakedness and rode into the town.

When she reached the market place her horse neighed, recognizing the face of its groom★ peeping out of a window. However, before he managed to see her nakedness, he was suddenly struck blind. Her journey completed, Godiva 'returned rejoicing to her husband, who considered it a miracle'.

Coventry is famous for its three spires, which are visible for miles around. Although two of the churches (Christchurch and St Michael) were flattened during wartime raids, their spires remained standing. The third spire belongs to Holy Trinity church, situated close to the cathedral. The spire dates from the seventeenth century and is 237 feet high.

There are four major medieval buildings in Coventry: Bablake School and Bond's Hospital, Ford's Hospital, St John's Hospital and St Mary's Guildhall.

The guildhall was built in 1342 for the Guild of St Mary. It was enlarged after the amalgamation of four guilds in 1394, and became the most powerful in Coventry. The guildhall became its headquarters. By the early sixteenth century the guilds began to decline. When they were suppressed in 1547 the hall came into the possession of the corporation, for the city had been incorporated in 1345 by Edward III. Since then it has been used as the town hall.

St John's Hospital, or the old grammar school, in Hales Street was founded in the twelfth century to provide accommodation for poor wayfarers. After the Dissolution of the Monasteries it was bought by John Hales, who converted it into a grammar school. It continued as such until 1885.

Ford's Hospital was founded in 1529 by William Ford, a wealthy merchant of Coventry. This attractive timber-framed building suffered severe bomb damage during the war but has since been repaired.

Leofric's foundation of the monastery attracted not only pilgrims but also merchants and craftsmen. The growth and prosperity of Coventry were also due to a number of charters and privileges bestowed on the town by the Earls of Chester and Henry II: one guaranteeing that merchants could trade in peace, another offering settlers free rent for two years from the moment they started to build.

At the time of the Domesday Book Coventry was a modest farming

★ The story as told by Matthew of Westminster (quoted by Burbidge) in the fourteenth century; in another version, Tom is a tailor.

community. By the end of the fourteenth century it was the fourth city in England (after London, York and Bristol) and the midland centre of the woollen industry. It was also noted for the production of caps, soap, needles and leather goods.

The city became so rich that a wall, just over two miles in length and over two yards thick, was built around it for defence. According to John Speed's map of 1610, the wall had twenty fortified towers and twelve gates. It was demolished in 1662 on the orders of Charles II; it had been a Parliamentary stronghold in the Civil War and he felt that anti-Royalist supporters might be tempted to make use of its defences in the future. Parts of the wall can still be found today.

A number of medieval streets have partly survived. These include Spon Street, Cook Street, Much Park Street and Bayley Lane, which runs alongside the fourteenth-century guildhall of St Mary and the ruins of the old cathedral.

Bond's Hospital, in Hill Street, stands behind the church of St John and was also an almshouse. It was founded by Thomas Bond, a Coventry draper. Close by is Bablake School, a half-timbered Tudor building, which was endowed by Thomas Wheatley in 1563. The school was founded in 1359 by the guild of St John, closed in 1548, when the guild was dissolved, re-opened by the town corporation in 1560 and moved to other premises in 1890.

After the decline in the wool and cloth industry in the seventeenth century, Coventry became a major producer of watches and ribbons and, later, sewing-machines and bicycles. After 1896, when Daimler opened a car factory here, the city expanded rapidly and by the mid twentieth century its prosperity was almost entirely based on the car industry.

When war was declared in 1939 many car firms changed over to aircraft manufacture and the production of armaments. Inevitably the city became a prime target for the German bombers. After sporadic air raids in August 1940, there occurred in October a series of seven intense raids, culminating in the attack on the night of 14 November when the cathedral was hit. Never before had an inhabited city been so devastated by an air raid.

The ruins of the old cathedral, with its charred and blackened wooden altar cross, were not pulled down, but were left standing as a memorial shrine to be incorporated later, by Sir Basil Spence, into the design of the new cathedral. On the exterior wall are giant bronze figures of St Michael and the Devil, by Sir Jacob Epstein. The interior contains works by major twentieth-century artists, including John Piper, Graham Sutherland and John Hutton.

As J.B. Priestley observed, in 1933, Coventry 'seems to have acquired the trick of keeping up with the times, a trick that many of our industrial cities find hard to learn'.

COVENTRY TO KENILWORTH

Once the Avon has passed under Ryton Bridge, it turns abruptly and meanders southwards past a bird sanctuary and Coventry Airport to Bubbenhall.

When Sir Arthur Thomas Quiller-Couch, known under the pseudonym of Q, canoed down this stretch of the Avon in the late nineteenth century, he remarked that the 'freakish stream went round and round, all meanders with never a forthright, narrowing, shallowing, casting up here a snag and there a thicket of reeds. And round and round for miles our canoe followed it, as a puppy chases his own tail; yet Bubbenhall was not, nor any glimpse of Bubbenhall.'

Despite Q's seemingly endless paddling, Bubbenhall is less than two miles, as the crow flies, from Ryton-on-Dunsmore. It is an attractive village, situated on a hill, with new houses tastefully designed to blend in with the old red-brick and timber-framed buildings. One of its charms is the abundance of trees in the streets, particularly the broad cul-de-sac leading to the church of St Giles and the river, which is lined with magnificent horse-chestnuts lit with lanterns of white flowers in spring.

The Avon flows past the site of a former mill, now occupied by a large, modern house, and then suddenly turns north towards Baginton, where there was once a castle, and just as suddenly resumes its south-westerly course at Bubbenhall Bridge. Ireland called it 'Broken Bridge' and added that 'its perfect state of repair would rather lead a conjecture that its proper appellation should have been Brooks Bridge'.

Half a mile downstream, the river passes under Cloud Bridge (the name is derived from the Saxon word *Clude*, signifying a rocky situation) and enters Stoneleigh Park, where ancient oaks are all that remain of the once great Forest of Arden.

In spring the woods are bright with primroses, violets, wood anemones and bluebells. The park contains badgers, foxes and deer, including the muntjak, or barking deer, the smallest deer in the United Kingdom.

Little has changed since Thorne's description of the river scene nearly a century and a half ago:

The stream meanders with a genial murmur through fertile meads, between banks, at one moment sloping so gently into its waters, that the ripple from the faintest breeze washes over the

The thirteenth-century church of St Giles, Bubbenhall
The river, shaded by trees, skirts the foot of the hill and passes the site of a mill which once belonged to the monks at Kenilworth Priory. The mill was demolished in 1964.

daisies that bedeck them; and presently starting up steep, broken, with an old willow above, whose rugged roots, bared by the winter's floods, now afford a support to the pink convolvulus, and all form a picture that gazes lovingly at its reflection in the dark mirror below.

Stareton, a small hamlet with attractive red-brick and timber-framed houses, takes its name, according to Dugdale, from *Stoure*, meaning a stream. Nearby is Stare Bridge, which is in fact two bridges bearing the same name. Ireland mentions a 'stone structure, built across the Avon, consisting of three arches, erected in 1674', but the present three-arched bridge is dated 1929. Ireland omits any reference to the older and more interesting late medieval bridge near by. Built of stone, it consists of nine stepped arches, only three of which span the river, with cutwaters in between. It once carried the main road over the Avon but since the road was diverted over the modern bridge, it has been used as a farm crossing.

The fields north of the bridge overlook the sprawling showground complex of the National Agricultural Centre, the annual venue for the Royal Show; on them graze a rare and ancient breed of White Park cattle, which were once used as draught animals and as sacrificial offerings by the Druids.

As the Avon loops around the permanent buildings, arenas and stands of the NAC it is joined, at Sowe Mouth, by the River Sowe, which flows south from Coventry.

To the west of the eight-arched Sowe Bridge, half a mile up the Sowe, lies the unspoilt village of Stoneleigh, or *Stanlei*, as it was anciently called. It is a small river-crossing settlement situated on high ground and containing a pleasing variety of stone, red-brick and timber-framed buildings. In the centre of the village, situated on a raised green under the leafy shade of a large chestnut tree, is a blacksmith's forge dated 1851. Opposite the forge is a row of red sandstone almshouses, bearing the date 1594, and near by stands a splendid black and white half-timbered manor-house, overlooking the church and the sloping meadows and woods of the Sowe valley.

The Blacksmith's Forge, Stoneleigh village
The red-brick building, with its tall chimney-stacks, has a large blue-brick horseshoe built into the western wall. The forge is still in operation today. In folklore blacksmiths are closely associated with the devil. In one Warwickshire legend they are linked to St Egwin, Bishop of Worcester. Because they refused to stop work on Sundays, he cursed them and, it is reputed, they grew devil-like tails.

The River Sowe near its confluence with the Avon, Stoneleigh

The red sandstone church of St Mary the Virgin dates from the twelfth century and underwent extensive alterations during the fourteenth century. Later additions included a vestry, a belfry and the Leigh Chapel.

The stone used for the building of the church and almshouses was quarried from Motslow Hill, on the opposite side of the river. It is thought to be an ancient site of fortification.

Once the Avon has received the waters of the

The River at Ashow

Welsh Way, the ancient track along which cattle and sheep were driven from Wales to the markets of the Midlands.

The bridge – which is said to be haunted by the figure of a woman – carries the busy A452 from Royal Leamington Spa over the Avon to Kenilworth and the red sandstone ruins of its once magnificent castle.

CHAPTER 4

KENILWORTH

At the time of the Norman Conquest Kenilworth was a small farming settlement in the Forest of Arden. According to the Domesday Book it was called *Chinewrde* and was held by Richard the forester, who was in the service of William the Conqueror. Kenilworth belonged to the king and was part of his manor at Stoneleigh. *Chinewrde* is an Old English word which is thought to mean 'the farm of a woman named Cynehild'. Later it became known as *Kenildewurde*, which could be derived from 'Cynehild' or 'Kenelm', a Saxon king of Mercia. The suffix of 'worth', which means an enclosed place or homestead, suggests that there may have been a fortress within the settlement.

Henry I gave the manor of Kenilworth to his chamberlain and treasurer, Geoffrey de Clinton, early in the twelfth century. De Clinton divided the land into two portions: the larger he donated for the foundation of an Augustinian priory; the smaller he reserved for a castle with its attendant park and chase.

The priory grew extremely wealthy and eventually became the Abbey of St Mary the Virgin. It was destroyed by Henry VIII at the Dissolution and its possessions were forfeited to the Crown. Its ruins are situated in Abbey Fields a short distance east of the castle.

The first castle was built of wood and sited on a knoll of rock and gravel, which was protected on all sides by marshland. These natural fortifications were improved by damming the nearby streams and flooding the low-lying land to leave the castle standing in defensive isolation on an island surrounded by water.

Castle Hill, leading to the High Street, Kenilworth

Aerial view of Kenilworth Castle

The wooden castle was replaced by one built of stone in the late twelfth century and enlarged in the reign of King John.

In the middle of the thirteenth century Henry III gave the castle to his sister, Eleanor, and her husband, Simon de Montfort, Earl of Leicester, who later led the barons in their war against the king. Kenilworth refused to surrender after de Montfort was killed in the battle of Evesham on the 4 August 1265, and in the following year the castle was besieged. The king arrived in person and he may have set up camp in the vicinity of Castle Green and Castle Hill. In fact, since the defenders had powerful catapult-type weapons, it is more likely that the main camp was sited much further away from the castle.

In the end, it was disease and starvation that forced the garrison to surrender, on 13 December 1266, after almost nine months of resistance.

Henry III gave the castle to his younger son, Edmund, and for over a hundred years it was the stronghold of the Earls of Lancaster. Subsequent construction work, however, concentrated more on comfort and pleasure.

In 1326, Henry, the third earl, brought Edward II to the castle as a prisoner and it was here that the king was forced to sign his abdication. He remained in Kenilworth for three months before being taken to Berkeley Castle, where he was murdered. After the abdication of Edward II, his son became Edward III.

When the male line of Lancaster came to an end in 1361, Edward III's fourth son, John of Gaunt, came into possession of the castle through his wife. He was immediately created Earl and, a year later, Duke of Lancaster.

John of Gaunt was responsible for the rebuilding of the Great Hall and private apartments. These alterations turned the castle into a palace.

When John of Gaunt's son became King Henry IV, in 1399, Kenilworth became Crown property until it was given to John Dudley, Duke of Northumberland, in 1553. Shortly afterwards the duke was executed and the castle reverted to the Crown.

Robert Dudley, the duke's son and heir, was granted the castle by Elizabeth I in 1563 and the following year he was created Earl of Leicester. He was the queen's favourite, born on exactly the same day (7 September 1533) as she.

The story of Dudley's ambition to marry Elizabeth was made famous by Sir Walter Scott in his novel *Kenilworth*, published in 1821. *Kenilworth* is based on the tragic fate of Amy Robsart, whom, according to Scott, Dudley had married secretly and installed at Cumnor Place, an old country house near Oxford. In reality, the marriage had been publicly celebrated in the reign of Edward VI. But, for the purpose of the novel, Dudley is forced to conceal his marriage from the jealous queen.

Weaving fact with fiction, Scott makes Dudley believe that his wife has been unfaithful and orders her to be killed. Too late, he learns that the accusations are false, for by then Amy has fallen through a trap-door and plunged to her death.

The real Amy also met her death in suspicious circumstances. She died on 8 September 1560 as a result of falling down a flight of stairs and breaking her neck. Gossip had it that she had been murdered by Dudley so that he would be free to marry Elizabeth.

The Queen visited Kenilworth on a number of occasions but the most memorable and the best recorded was her visit of 1575. No expense was spared in the festivities: spectacular aquatic displays, feasting, fireworks, music, masques and song. Clearly, everyone living within miles would have been irresistibly drawn to the celebrations.

At the time the castle was at its most magnificent, surrounded by a huge defensive lake. The highlight of the queen's stay was a water-pageant where a large mermaid floated across the lake carrying a trumpeter. Moored nearby was a huge dolphin with a number of musicians in its belly and a singer on its back. If, as is possible, Shakespeare was at the celebrations, the experience is echoed, many years later, in *A Midsummer Night's Dream*:

> *Thou rememb'rest*
> *Since once I sat upon a promontory,*
> *And heard a mermaid on a dolphin's back*
> *Uttering such dulcet and harmonious breath*
> *That the rude sea grew civil at her song,*
> *And certain stars shot madly from their spheres*
> *To hear the sea-maid's music.*

To all those who saw the Earl of Leicester and Queen Elizabeth over those memorable weeks it seemed certain that a wedding was in the offing. However, during his rise to stardom, the earl had made many political enemies and the queen was well aware of the friction their union would cause. Duty dictated that the stability of the realm should come before personal happiness. Reason, in the end, ruled her heart.

The dramatic ruins of Kenilworth Castle on the north-western outskirts of the town

In 1575 Robert Dudley, Earl of Leicester, entertained Queen Elizabeth I at the castle for seventeen days. The lavish scale of the celebrations fuelled speculation that a wedding was in the offing, but Elizabeth remained unmarried, and she never returned to Kenilworth.

Shortly afterwards Leicester married again, much to the queen's displeasure. After his death in 1588, the castle passed to his brother and then to Leicester's son by his second marriage, Sir Robert Dudley. Eventually, the property was seized by the Crown.

After the battle of Edge Hill in 1642, the castle was taken by the Parliamentarians and, at the end of the Civil War, Parliament ordered its destruction. The Earl of Monmouth successfully petitioned that the castle should be 'slighted with as little spoil to the dwellinghouse as might be'.

The vast red sandstone ruins of one of the most glorious and historic castles in England were given to the nation in 1937. The castle is now managed by English Heritage, Historic Buildings & Monuments Commission for England.

KENILWORTH TO ROYAL LEAMINGTON SPA

Chesford Bridge and the Chesford Grange Hotel lie one mile south of Kenilworth. Near by, the Avon is joined by the tiny Cattle Brook before sweeping past arable fields and mixed woodland to Blackdown Mill.

The mill buildings were erected in the eighteenth and nineteenth centuries, the oldest part being the three-storey brick structure, to which has been added a large wooden extension housing the waterwheel.

Once the property of the monks of Coombe Abbey, the mill was in operation until the mid 1920s, when it was driven by a steam engine. Today, the building is the premises of an antique dealer and furniture restorer.

Above the mill stands the little hamlet of Hill Wootton, which contains a large manor-house and some fine red-brick and timber-framed houses. A mile to the west lies the sprawling village of Leek Wootton which, unlike its hill-top neighbour, possesses a church.

Close to the large roundabout, south of Wootton Court, is a small road named North Woodloes. At the very end of the cul-de-sac a narrow footpath, running alongside a tall hedgerow, climbs high above the noisy bypass and on to the wooded summit of Blacklow Hill, the site of Gaveston's Cross.

From the sandstone cliff of Blacklow Hill the view – spanning the Warwick bypass – includes the Avon as it weaves its easy way through pleasant meadows and shady trees to Guy's Cliffe, the setting for one of the most popular legends of English medieval romance.

GUY'S CLIFFE

At Guy's Cliffe the Avon quickens its pace, as if aware that the spot is haunted. The river hurries past the so-called Saxon Mill and tumbles over a weir to gather in a dark and treacherous pool where many have drowned.

On its western bank it passes high sandstone cliffs shrouded in trees, above which tower the mysterious, overgrown ruins of what was once an impressive Georgian mansion built about 1751 for Samuel Greatheed. In 1826 the house descended to the Percy family, who kept it until 1946, when it was sold and allowed to fall into decay.

The Avon near Guy's Cliffe

According to the historian John Rous, who was chaplain of the chapel here until his death in 1491, the site was first selected by St Dubricius as a place of worship and, once an oratory had been built, it was dedicated to St Mary Magdalen.

It is also recorded that a hermit occupied one of the caves which have been carved out of the soft sandstone rock until at least the end of the fourteenth century.

At the foot of the cliff is a large but shallow cave,

known as 'Guy's Cave'; like the cliff itself, it takes its name from Guy of Warwick, one of the great heroes of medieval romance.

His exploits were first put in writing by an Anglo-Norman poet in the twelfth century and were soon accepted as history.

The story is related by the Countess of Warwick in *Warwick Castle and its Earls*. Guy was the son of Siward, a Northumbrian nobleman who had lost his lands in a quarrel; he headed south seeking to mend his fortune, and his manner and ability so impressed Rohand, Earl of Warwick, that he appointed him as his personal steward.

Guy fell in love with the earl's daughter, Felice, and resolved to try and win her hand by performing many heroic and noble deeds.

Taking up his arms, he left Warwick to travel overseas in search of fame: he went to Normandy, where he rescued a damsel in distress, and to Germany, where he won the hand of the emperor's daughter in a tournament, but when he explained his love for Felice, the obligation was dismissed and treasures were heaped upon him.

Felice, however, was not impressed and on his return to Warwick Castle she sent him away to 'seek more adventures'.

On Dunsmore Heath lived a monstrous creature, known as the Dun Cow, which destroyed every living thing it encountered. It was huge, 'beyond the ordinary size of other cattle, six yards in length,

Gaveston Cross, Blacklow Hill
Hidden amidst the trees, about two hundred yards into the wood, this monument marks the spot where Piers Gaveston, the favourite of Edward II, is supposed to have been executed. The inscription on the cross is far from complimentary, either to Gaveston or to Edward II: 'In the hollow of this rock, was beheaded on the 1st. day of July, 1312, by barons lawless as himself, Piers Gaveston, Earl of Cornwall; the minion of a hateful king: in life and death, a memorable instance of misrule.'

and four high, with large sharp horns and fiery eyes, of a dun colour'.

The beast was ravaging a hundred head of cattle

when Guy rode up and, without a moment's hesitation, attacked. After a bitter struggle, he hit the creature with such force under the ear that it died in 'a weltering stream of blood'.

King Athelstan, having heard of this tremendous feat, conferred a knighthood upon Guy and 'caused one of the cow's ribs to be hung up in Warwick Castle to his fame'. It, or the rib of some other large animal, is still there today.

Sir Guy now left to pursue further exploits abroad. His fame spread throughout the known world: he relieved the city of Byzantium, which was beseiged by Turks; he killed a 'fiery dragon' which was attacking a 'fierce lion' and the lion, in gratitude, licked the hero's feet; he slew a boar whose head weighed 'almost an hundredweight'.

Eventually, after many similarly heroic deeds, he returned to England.

Before Sir Guy could go to Felice, King Athelstan summoned him to York. Apparently, a dreadful dragon, inhabiting a cave in Northumberland, was wreaking havoc on the surrounding countryside. Sir Guy quickly dispatched the beast, which proved to be over thirty feet long, and, heaped with 'many rich presents', finally went home to Warwick.

The Earl Rohand gave him the hand of Felice and they were married 'with much joy and triumph'. The earl died soon afterwards and Sir Guy inherited his estate. Athelstan made him Earl of Warwick 'by which title he was ranked with other lords and peers and in favour with all men' (Drewry).

Sir Guy had achieved everything his heart had desired. He had fame, a title, lands and wealth. More importantly, Felice was now his wife. But he had discovered that wanting and having were two different things. At the height of his success he found himself unhappy; his conscience bade him 'repent of all his former sins, and his youthful time, spent in the behalf of women'. He resolved to leave Warwick and travel to the Holy Land on a pilgrimage.

Felice, sensing that something was seriously wrong, questioned him. 'Ah! Felice,' said he, 'I have spent much time in honouring thee, and to win thy favour, but never spared one minute for my soul's health in honouring the Lord' (Drewry).

It was Felice's turn to be heartbroken. After they had exchanged rings, Sir Guy 'departed like a stranger from his own habitation, taking neither money nor scrip with him . . . vowing never to fight more but in a just cause'.

Not surprisingly, he had many more adventures and fought many more battles. This time, though, he fought not for the love of a woman but for the love of God.

As the years dragged by, Felice remained true to

her long-departed husband and devoted her life to helping the poor and needy. She followed Guy's progress through the stories that reached her of his deeds. She heard how he slew the giant Amerand; how he overcame the Danish champion, Colbrand, and rescued King Athelstan from certain defeat at Winchester. Then she heard no more. There were no new stories and no more news. She presumed him dead.

Felice grew old. She continued to give alms, in

person, to the beggars that assembled daily outside the castle gate. One day a stranger showed her a ring – the very one that she had given Sir Guy all those years ago. She was overcome with emotion and asked the stranger to explain how it had come into his possession.

The stranger led her out of the castle, across the snow-clad fields and down to the river beside the sandstone cliffs. He stopped before the entrance to a large cave, in which Sir Guy lay dying: 'When she came to the cave, she embraced his weak body, and sent forth abundance of tears, between joy and sorrow.'

Sir Guy explained that he was well pleased with her 'chaste life and pious doings' since his departure and that, unrecognized, he had himself received alms from her hand at the castle gate. Felice did not understand. In the words of the Countess of Warwick:

'Heaven knows,' he said, 'I love no earthly thing like myself, but the care of my immortal soul made me despise all earthly felicities, but willing to see thee once more before my life was spent, I sent the ring according to my promise, that thou mightest come and close my dying eyes'.

And so, in Felice's arms, he died.

Unable to bear the pain of being parted yet again, Felice climbed the sandstone cliffs and leapt to her

Guy's Cliffe House ruins
Perched on the top of a high sandstone cliff, the ghostly ruins of Guy's Cliffe House tower above the Avon. The once impressive Georgian mansion was built in about 1751 for Samuel Greatheed. Sarah Siddons (née Kemble), the great actress, became a lady's maid at the house in 1772 after a quarrel with her father over a fellow-actor, William Siddons, whom she married the following year in Coventry.

death. Her body plunged into the icy river and the waters of the Avon carried her away – and into legend.

———

In the fourteenth-century chapel at Guy's Cliffe is a large medieval stone sculpture of Sir Guy and at Warwick Castle can be found other relics reputed to have belonged to the heroic knight, including a massive porridge pot and a great two-handed sword.

Old Milverton, standing on a low hill across the meadows, was once a small village, but is gradually becoming part of the expanding suburbs of Royal Leamington Spa.

CHAPTER 5

ROYAL LEAMINGTON SPA

In 1838, twenty-six days after Victoria's coronation, Leamington Spa was granted its royal charter and became the world's first royal town. A hundred and fifty years later, on 24 March 1988, Queen Elizabeth II unveiled a plaque at the town hall. This was one of a long line of royal visits to the town stretching back to 1819, when the Prince Regent, later King George IV, permitted the newly built Regent Hotel to be named after him.

Named after the River Leam which flows through its centre, Leamington was a small hamlet at the time of the Domesday survey, with two mills and lands 'two hides in extent' (about 240 acres). It became Leamington Priors when the manor was given to Kenilworth Priory by Geoffrey de Clinton, whose father had founded the priory in the twelfth century.

When the Abbey of St Mary, Kenilworth (for the priory had been raised in status), was demolished at the Dissolution, the lands became the property of the Crown. Elizabeth I granted Leamington Priors to Ambrose Dudley, Earl of Warwick, but after his death the estate reverted to the Crown. James I gave the estate and Warwick Castle to Sir Fulke Greville, later Lord Brooke, and from then on the lands passed through various ownerships.

The first written reference to the spring at Leamington Priors was probably made by John Rous in the fifteenth century. From the end of the seventeenth century, the medicinal properties of the spring waters were noted by various medical writers. But William Abbotts, landlord of the Dog Inn, and Benjamin Satchwell, a cobbler, are given the credit for the founding of the spa. For several years they endeavoured to find a way of exploiting the medicinal properties of the waters. By chance they discovered a new spring on Abbotts's land. After the water had been analysed by Dr Kerr of Northampton, whose findings were extremely favourable, the first baths were opened in 1786.

At the time Leamington Priors had 'the appearance of a rural and retired village' (Field) and 'the only houses of accommodation were two small inns, the Dog, and the Bowling Green' (Moncrieff), and a few humble cottages. The population was about three hundred but it slowly grew as the waters attracted more and more visitors.

As the reputation of the curative properties of the waters increased, more wells were sunk and Leamington became a fashionable place to live. Within the forty years from 1811 the population rose from 543 to over 15,000.

Most of the early development was on the south side of the River Leam. By 1813 the main buildings included Abbotts' Baths, the New Inn, Lord Aylesford's Well, which covered the original spring, Robbins' Baths, Wise's Baths, Read's Baths, the Theatre and the Albion Hotel.

In 1808 a new development was initiated on the north bank, mainly due to the increasing difficulty of purchasing land in the southern part of the town.

The new town was planned roughly in the shape of a square with the wide main street, the Parade, intersected at right angles by Cross Street (now Regent Street) and Warwick Street. To this were added side streets, terraces, squares and crescents. By 1830 there were over one hundred streets containing over one thousand houses.

The most important building in the development of Leamington as a spa town was the Pump Room, opened in 1814. It was designed by C.S. Smith in the classical style with a long Tuscan colonnade, which still survives, though extensively altered. Above the colonnade the original name of the 'Royal Pump Room and Baths' remains.

As the reputation of the spa town grew it attracted many distinguished visitors including the Prince Regent, Princess Augusta, the Duke and Duchess

1 Newbold Terrace, Royal Leamington Spa
This house has an unusual two-storeyed porch, consisting of two pairs of fluted Ionic columns with similar columns supporting a balcony above. The upper pillars are beautifully fretted and support a pierced architrave with a pediment on top.

of Bedford, the Duke and Duchess of Gloucester and the Crown Prince and Princess of Denmark. Princess Victoria, later Queen Victoria, arrived with her mother in 1830.

Many of these visitors were patients of Dr Henry Jephson, who first came to Leamington in 1819 and settled permanently in the town eleven years later. When he died in 1878 his obituary in the *Leamington Courier* called him 'The Father of Leamington' and claimed that 'this Spa of Leamington owes its fame chiefly to Dr Jephson'.

Although others contributed to the success of the spa, it was Jephson's reputation as a physician and philanthropist that brought royalty, aristocracy and the famous flocking to the town. Unfortunately, illness forced Jephson to retire from his practice in 1848 and by the end of the year, at the age of fifty, he was completely blind. The following year his statue, housed within a classical temple, was unveiled in the centre of the Jephson Gardens.

In addition to its parks and gardens, Royal Leamington Spa is noted for its broad tree-lined avenues, white-painted terraces, excellent shopping facilities and a wealth of Georgian, Regency and early Victorian architecture. During the 1830s William Thomas designed some pleasant streets in the town, including Lansdowne Crescent and Lansdowne Circus.

The town hall, built in 1882–4 by J. Cundall, is of red brick and brown stone. Near the main entrance is a large statue of Queen Victoria, which was shifted one inch from its original position by a Second World War bomb.

Nathaniel Hawthorne, the American novelist, lived at 10 Lansdowne Circus while writing *Our Old Home*, published in 1863, and called it 'one of the cosiest nooks in England or in the world'. Charles Dickens came to the town in 1855 and 1862 and parts of *Dombey and Son* were set in the Pump Room and nearby Holly Walk.

Leamington has expanded considerably since the nineteenth century: recent development within the town centre has led to the demolition of a number of old buildings; industrial estates, factories and business parks have grown on the outskirts; the suburbs have spread in every direction and those to the west now merge with the suburbs of Warwick. Yet the town has still managed to preserve much of the architectural elegance of its golden age.

Lansdowne Crescent, Royal Leamington Spa

The classically designed houses of Lansdowne Crescent and Lansdowne Circus, built by William Thomas in the 1830s, are notable for the delicate fretted ironwork of their verandas.

ROYAL LEAMINGTON SPA TO WARWICK

*Aerial view of Royal
Leamington Spa*

From the open meadows below Old Milverton, the Avon is suddenly squeezed, for about a mile, between the conjoining houses and factories of Royal Leamington Spa and Warwick. It receives the waters of the Leam near Emscote Bridge and, threading its way through urban development, it passes under an aqueduct – carrying the Grand Union Canal – and a railway line, to emerge in St Nicholas's Park, Warwick.

Castle Bridge, built in 1793, stands at the southern end of the park and from it there is a picture-postcard view of the broad Avon, the ruins of the old bridge and, soaring above them both, the magnificent medieval castle of Warwick.

*Warwick Castle with the
River Avon in flood*

CHAPTER 6
WARWICK

Warwick is situated on a rocky hill overlooking the Avon. Although there is evidence of Neolithic occupation, the name is Saxon in origin. The earliest form of Warwick is *Waerinc Wic*, meaning 'the dwellings by the weir'. The settlement may have been established in the sixth or early seventh century by the tribe of the Hwicce.

Warwick was unable to develop as a major centre for trade: the main routes bypassed the town and the Avon was only navigable further downstream. Its importance, therefore, was due entirely to its strategic position.

In 914, King Alfred the Great's daughter, Ethelfleda, built a fortress on the rock. A large mound within the castle walls is still known as Ethelfleda's Mound. By the eleventh century, after the Norman Conquest, a wooden motte and bailey castle had been built. In the twelfth and thirteenth centuries the wooden tower was replaced with one of stone, and the walls were strengthened. Guy's Tower and Caesar's Tower were built in the fourteenth century.

Except for the side facing the Avon, the outer walls are protected by a waterless moat. The entrance has a gatehouse with a drawbridge, portcullis and murder holes. The gatehouse also has a barbican, built on the other side of the moat, making entry even more hazardous.

During the eleventh century Warwick was governed by Turchill, son of Alwine, an Anglo-Saxon earl. Turchill was called 'The Traitor' because he failed to go to Harold's assistance at the battle of Hastings. He was rewarded by William the Conqueror and made the custodian of the newly fortified town of

Ethelfleda's Mound, Warwick Castle, named after the daughter of Alfred the Great, who built a fortress here as protection against the Danes

Warwick. After Turchill's death, William Rufus gave the castle to Henry de Beauchamp, a Norman, and created him Earl of Warwick.

Warwick was by far the most famous of all the castles of the Midlands, and its powerful earls have been involved in most of the influential events in the nation's history. They fought in the Hundred Years War at Agincourt, Crécy and Poitiers. They were prominent in the wars of Stephen and of Edward II, the Wars of the Roses and the Civil War.

Guy de Beauchamp, the tenth Earl of Warwick, was party to the trial and execution of Piers Gaveston, the favourite of Edward II, who was beheaded on Blacklow Hill, in 1312 (see p. 61).

The greatest of the Beauchamps was Richard, the thirteenth Earl and the trusted friend of Henry V. He held the office of 'Captain of Calais' and superintended the trial and execution of Joan of Arc. After his death in 1439 the title and property passed to his son, and then to his daughter, Anne Beauchamp, who married Richard Neville, son of the Earl of Salisbury. Neville was known as 'The Kingmaker' because of his power and influence in the struggle for the crown between the rival dynasties of York and Lancaster. At the same time he had two kings in captivity: Henry VI in the Tower of London and Edward IV at Warwick Castle. He was killed at the battle of Barnet in 1471.

Neville was succeeded by George Plantagenet, Duke of Clarence, the younger brother of King Edward IV and of Richard, Duke of Gloucester, who later became Richard III. After Clarence was caught plotting to overthrow his brother the king, he was imprisoned and privately executed in the Tower of London in 1478. According to Shakespeare, he was drowned in a butt of malmsey wine.

Clarence's son, Edward Plantagenet, spent most of his life in prison until he too was executed, as the principal Yorkist claimant to the throne, in 1499. The castle and estates were forfeited to the Crown.

In 1547, Edward VI granted the earldom to John Dudley, his chief minister, who also became Duke of Northumberland. The king died six years later and Mary, Henry VIII's daughter by Catherine of Aragon, inherited the throne. She was an ardent Catholic and she determined to restore Catholicism to England. Dudley, who was a Protestant, was among those executed in the persecutions that followed. He left five sons and two daughters. Of these, the third son, Robert Dudley, became the Earl of Leicester. The second son, Ambrose, after the death of his elder brother John and fifteen months' imprisonment, became the twenty-first earl. Ambrose was party to the execution of Mary, Queen of Scots; at her trial, she pleaded with him 'not to believe all things that he had heard of her'. He was known as 'The Good Earl' because of his benevolence to the people of Warwick.

In 1539, John Leland observed of Warwick:

The beauty and glory of the town, is in two streets, whereof the one is called the High Street, and goeth from the East Gate to the West, having a right goodly cross in the middle of it; the other crosseth the middle of it, making a *quadrivium*, and goeth from north to south.

The southern arm of this cross is Castle Street. Although it is now blocked by the walls of the castle grounds, it originally ran to the east of the castle and across the Avon towards London. Oken's House, in Castle Street, is a sixteenth-century timber-framed building once owned by Thomas Oken, a great benefactor to the town, who died in the house on 29 July 1573. It now houses a museum of dolls.

The medieval bridge of fourteen arches, now in ruins, was superseded by Castle Bridge, built by George Greville, in 1793 and sited upstream. Mill Street with its medieval, Tudor and Georgian houses, was formerly the 'great eastern entrance into the town'. It is the best-preserved street of ancient buildings in Warwick and ends at the foot of the 147-feet-high Caesar's Tower.

On 12 August 1572, Queen Elizabeth came to the town and her visit was recorded in 'The Black Book of Warwick'.

She stayed in Warwick for a few days before visiting Robert Dudley at Kenilworth (see p. 56). On her return, Ambrose Dudley, Earl of Warwick, staged a great entertainment that culminated in a show of fireworks. Sadly, the display went wrong:

a ball of fire fell on a house at the end of the bridge, wherein one Henry Cowy, otherwise called Miller, dwelt, and set fire on the same house, the man and wife being both in bed and asleep. Which burned so as, before any rescue could be, the house and all things in it utterly perished, with much ado to save the man and woman . . . the fireballs and squibs cast up did fly quite over the Castle and

St Mary's Church, Warwick
In 1694 a fire raged through the town destroying properties and badly damaging St Mary's Church. The magnificent, richly decorated Beauchamp Chapel, built in 1443–64, fortunately survived. Among the architects who submitted plans for the rebuilding of the church was Sir Christopher Wren, but Sir William Wilson was selected and the work was carried out by the local Smith brothers.

into the midst of the town, falling down, some on houses, some in courts and backsides, and some in the streets, as far as almost of St Mary Church, to the great peril, or else great fear, of the inhabitants of this borough.

Lord Leycester's Hospital and St James's Chapel, Warwick

Founded by Robert Dudley, Earl of Leicester, in 1571, this beautiful timbered hospital stands beside the narrow West Gate of the town. On top of the long tunnelled archway, partly cut out of the solid rock, is the Chapel of St James, founded in the twelfth century and later rebuilt.

It is remarkable that the whole town did not go up in flames for the houses, built mainly of timber and thatch, were close together. In 1694 the inhabitants were not so lucky. A fire started in the centre of the town and destroyed two hundred and fifty properties before it was put out. It stopped short of the chancel of St Mary's Church but destroyed the aisle and nave.

After Queen Elizabeth I had returned to London Ambrose Dudley resumed the business of overseeing the day-to-day interests of the town. 'The Black Book of Warwick' illustrates many of the problems that took up his time, from the expulsion of a bigamist to the election of burgesses to represent the town in Parliament.

Despite his energetic character, the earl's later years were far from active. A

Oken's House, Castle Street, Warwick
This half-timbered Elizabethan house was the home of Thomas Oken, a wealthy mercer and great benefactor to the town. His death in 1573, and the bedside scuffle that broke out over the fact that he had drawn up not one will but two, are vividly described in 'The Black Book of Warwick'. Today the house is the home of the unique Joy Robinson collection of dolls.

leg wound he had received at Le Havre in 1563 constantly caused him trouble. In 1590 Anthony Bagot recorded that 'the Earl of Warwick had one of his legs cut off by the knee for the disease . . . called gangrene'. The operation killed him. Dudley was buried in the Beauchamp Chapel of St Mary's Church, Warwick, and the castle once more reverted to the Crown.

In 1604 the castle was given to Sir Fulke Greville by James I. In due course, the Grevilles were granted the title of Earl of Warwick and it remains with the family to this day.

Warwick Castle, however, was sold to Madame Tussaud's in November 1978. Today its function has changed from a fortress to an international tourist attraction, billed as one of the finest medieval castles in the land.

WARWICK TO STRATFORD-UPON-AVON

Francis Greville, first Earl Brooke and first Earl of Warwick, who made many improvements to the castle and grounds in the eighteenth century, built 'a noble lake from three hundred to six hundred feet broad, and a mile long'. This lake, named 'New Waters' on the Ordnance Survey map, was formed by the damming of a small stream which rises four miles to the south-east near the site of a Roman settlement on the Fosse Way at Chesterton.

The stream, which flows between Bishop's Tachbrook and Tachbrook Mallory, is referred to in the opening line of Walter Savage Landor's poem 'To Tacaea' as the 'brightest-eyed of Avon's train'.

After emerging from the lake considerably wider than it entered it, 'Tacaea' joins the Avon on the northern outskirts of Lodge Wood. Broadened by the weirs of Warwick Castle and swelled by the waters of the lake, the Avon follows the woods for about half a mile and, entering flat boggy land filled with reed-beds, it heads towards Longbridge.

The old hamlet and manor-house, together with a new housing development, are situated to the north-east of the huge Longbridge road junction. From here, the Avon glides through meadows and rushes over weirs to Barford Bridge.

When Ireland passed here at the end of the eighteenth century, the stone bridge was being built 'to supply the place of the old one, which by length of time had fallen to decay'.

Barford was the home of Joseph Arch (1826–1919), who founded the National Agricultural Workers Union in 1872 in order to improve the conditions of farm workers. He was born and died in a small cottage near the church of St Peter and on the main road there is a tavern named after him.

The oldest part of the church is the Perpendicular west tower, dating from the fourteenth century. The remainder was rebuilt in 1844 by R.C. Hussey and paid for by Miss Louisa Ann Ryland of nearby Sherbourne Manor.

Sherbourne is situated beside the Sherbourne Brook, 'a small trout stream' from which the village is said to derive its name.

The church of All Saints, built by Sir George Gilbert Scott in 1864, was also generously paid for by Miss Ryland. In addition, she paid for the rebuilding of most of the village in the Elizabethan style.

South-west of Sherbourne is Castle Hill, on which the 'little' castle of Fulbrook once stood. In

The Avon in the grounds of Warwick Castle
The river flows through landscaped grounds where peacocks strut around the lawns and cry for attention from the top of the high stone walls.

the fifteenth century, it was held by John, Duke of Bedford, third son of Henry IV, who, by enclosing Fulbrook Park, 'converted a formerly safe highway into a notorious haunt of robbers, who lay in wait for their victims behind the newly erected palings' (Levi Fox, in the Victoria County History, vol. 3).

In order to create the park the village of Fulbrook was destroyed. The church was demolished in the sixteenth century and all that is left of the parish today is a few scattered farms and a group of cottages on Sherbourne Hill.

The name of Fulbrook is supposed by Dugdale to refer to the small stream which runs down the hillside into the Avon.

The castle, built of stone and brick, was demolished in the reign of Henry VIII by Sir William Compton, who used the materials to build his mansion at Compton Wynyates, twelve miles away.

Hampton Wood, once belonging to Fulbrook Park, is situated on a hill above the west bank of the Avon. The wood provides a natural sanctuary for a wide variety of birds and wild animals and is now a WARNACT nature reserve. Shakespeare may have come here to escape from the noisy bustle of nearby Stratford-upon-Avon. In *The Two Gentlemen of Verona* he wrote:

> . . . *unfrequented woods,*
> *I better brook than flourishing peopled towns.*

> *Here can I sit alone, unseen of any*
> *And to the nightingale's complaining notes*
> *Tune my distresses and record my woes.*

After the Avon has received the waters of the Sherbourne Brook, it sweeps round Hampton Wood to Wasperton. The river banks are steep and high in places and provide an ideal site for the shy kingfisher to nest undisturbed by river traffic – the river is unnavigable above Alveston weir.

Weaving between rolling wooded hills, the Avon here becomes extremely shallow in parts and reeds and water-lilies abound. Willows mingle with hawthorn, beech and ash. Lush, flat, grazing meadows, liable to flooding, lie on either side of the river.

In the buttercup meadow by the river's edge at Wasperton stands a damaged aircraft propeller and beside it is a simple plaque which reads: 'This memorial was erected by the Stratford on Avon Aviation and Militaria Enthusiasts to the memory of the two Commonwealth air crews who died on this stretch of river 1942 and 1943 – Lest we Forget.'

The village of Wasperton lies on elevated ground above the Avon at the end of a no-through-road. The church of St John the Baptist, with its wooden bell turret, was built in 1843 by Sir George Gilbert Scott in the style of 1300. Almost hidden by tall trees, it lies behind Cedar House and is reached by a narrow footpath flanked by the high garden hedges of the adjacent houses.

South of St Peters, Church Lane, Barford

Manor House Farm, a red-brick and timber-framed building overlooking the open fields, dates from the fifteenth century, although the exterior is mostly eighteenth century.

Between Wasperton and Charlecote the eastern side of the Avon valley is scarred by extensive gravel and sand workings. Across the valley the eastern ridge of Copdock Hill gives way to the precipitous wall of trees known as Scar Bank. A short distance from its confluence with Thelsford

Brook the Avon divides, with Charlecote Mill on the eastern branch.

Cerlecote, as Charlecote was written in the Domesday Book, had two mills valued at 21s. in 1086. The present corn mill dates from the eighteenth century.

The village of Hampton Lucy lies close to the mill on the opposite bank of the Avon and was originally called Bishop's Hampton, having been owned by the bishops of Worcester. In 1557, after the Dissolution, the manor was granted to the Lucy family by Queen Mary and the name was changed to Hampton Lucy.

Most of the cottages were built in the early nineteenth century and one writer commented that 'A considerable degree of neatness marks the appearance of the cottages and each is distinguished by its particular number.' In addition to the more recent houses there are a number of older properties including the late-seventeenth-century rectory and Avonside, formerly the grammar school, founded in 1635.

The church of St Peter dates from 1826 and was built by the Reverend John Lucy 'not exactly on the same site' as the medieval church, which was demolished in the same year. It was designed by Thomas Rickman and is considered to be one of the earliest and best examples of the Gothic Revival.

The iron bridge spanning the Avon at the east end of the village was erected in 1829 and was cast at the

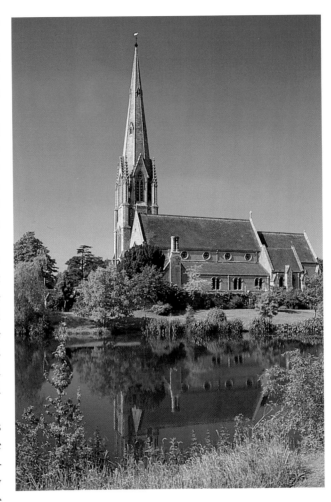

Church of All Saints, Sherbourne

Horseley Ironworks in Shropshire. It was built to replace 'a ford and wooden causeway for foot passengers'.

Just beyond the bridge the two branches of the river unite and, now much wider, the Avon courses through level green meadows to the deer-stocked park of Charlecote.

CHARLECOTE PARK

The Lucy family have lived at Charlecote for almost eight hundred years and are therefore one of the oldest county families still living in the same place. The estate was granted to Thurstan de Charlecote by Henry de Montfort towards the end of the twelfth century. Walter, his son, married Cicely, who is thought to have been a member of the great baronial family of Lucy of Cockermouth and Egremont in Cumberland, because their son was Sir William de Lucy.

For almost four hundred years the family lived in a moated manor-house lying on the eastern bank of the river, close to where the Avon is joined by the River Dene. In 1558 Sir Thomas Lucy decided to demolish it and build in its place a mansion designed in the shape of a capital E, in honour of the first Queen Elizabeth.

The gatehouse, constructed in 1550, dominates the entrance and, like the house, is built of rose-pink brick from the kilns at Hampton Lucy. The grounds landscaped by Lancelot 'Capability' Brown in 1760 and the mansion was altered and extended in the nineteenth century.

Leading from the park entrance to the gatehouse there was once a long avenue of ancient elms, a tree which was so common in the area that it was called the 'Warwickshire weed'. Unfortunately, the outbreak of Dutch elm disease in the late 1970s killed almost every elm in the county and all that now remains of the elms at Charlecote Park are their huge decaying stumps, displaying annual rings dating back hundreds of years. The avenue was replanted with the ornamental and fast-growing Turkey oak.

The open parkland at Charlecote, with its rich clumps of trees, is a haven for wildlife. It is enclosed by traditional split-oak fencing, said to have been used here since Elizabethan times. The park contains red and fallow deer and Jacob sheep, a rare breed introduced to Charlecote over two hundred years ago.

There is a tradition, persistent but unsubstantiated, that the young William Shakespeare was caught red-handed poaching deer from Charlecote Park. According to the legend, first recorded in the early eighteenth century, the park was well stocked with fallow deer (red deer were introduced later).

From his writings it is clear that Shakespeare's knowledge of hunting deer was considerable. He seemed to know more about driving deer into nets or shooting them with a crossbow than chasing

them with dogs for sport. In *King Henry VI, Part III*, he writes:

FIRST KEEPER *Under this thick-grown brake we'll shroud*
      ourselves;
   For through this laund anon the deer will come;
   And in this covert will we make our stand,
   Culling the principal of all the deer.

From *Love's Labour's Lost* it appears that, if he did poach deer, he preferred to kill them outright with a crossbow rather than let them suffer:

   Thus will I save my credit in the shoot:
   Not wounding, pity would not let me do't.

And in *As You Like It* he describes the plight of the injured animal:

   Under an oak whose antique root peeps out
   Upon the brook that brawls along this wood!
   To the which place a poor sequest'red stag,
   That from the hunter's aim had ta'en a hurt,
   Did come to languish.

Shakespeare was aware that, for the poacher, the hunter was also the hunted and the successful kill was accompanied by the thrill of outwitting the gamekeeper. In *Titus Andronicus* he writes:

Hampton Wood
The wood is now a WARNACT nature reserve and provides sanctuary for a wide variety of birds and wild animals. It is an ancient oak and hazel woodland which, in spring and early summer, is carpeted with bluebells and primroses. Other wild flowers found here include the foul-smelling yellow archangel, the poisonous dog's mercury and the pretty red campion.

What, hast not thou full often struck a doe,
And borne her cleanly by the keeper's nose?

Although Shakespeare reveals a thorough knowledge of poaching in his plays, there is no evidence that he put it into practice, despite the reference to 'a dozen white luces' in *The Merry Wives of Windsor*; luces were pike (fish) and, coincidentally or not, appeared on the Lucy family's coat of arms.

According to the legend, when Shakespeare was caught he was hauled before Sir Thomas Lucy, who was not only the lord of the manor but also a magistrate. It is said that because of this unfortunate incident Shakespeare was forced to leave Stratford-upon-Avon and go to London and that later, as an act of revenge, he caricatured Sir Thomas as Justice

Ancient willows beside the Avon at Wasperton
When Showell reached Wasperton in about 1900, he remarked on the 'awkward-looking' pollard willows. A few of the trees remain and, although old and cracking, they are still being polled. Crack willows can be found all along the river from here to Tewkesbury and, having long penetrating roots, they play an important role in the prevention of river-bank erosion.

Shallow and thereby made him the laughing-stock of London's playhouses. It is also reported that the Lucy family were so annoyed that in their library copy of the *Merry Wives* they tore out the offending pages.

In 1572 Elizabeth I stayed at Charlecote for two nights. Her stay is commemorated by a coat of arms over the Renaissance porch of the house in which the arms of England are supported by a lion on one side and a dragon on the other.

Exhilarates the Meads and to his Bed
Hele's gentle current wooes, by Lucy's hand
In every graceful Ornament attired,
And worthier, such, to share his liquid Realms.

From Charlecote Park the Avon, writes Ireland, 'winding its pleasant course, affords a beautiful and extensive view of the Feldon of Warwickshire, called the Vale of Red Horse'.

The pleasant village of Alveston is situated within a loop in the river; in the early nineteenth century it was called by Dr Perry the 'Montpelier of England', on account of the 'salubrity of the air'. It contains some extremely expensive houses with gardens running down to the water's edge. The Ferry Inn serves as a reminder that there was once a ferry here; in the Domesday Book it is recorded that there were also three mills. The parish stretches along the southern bank of the river to Stratford-upon-Avon.

Just within the eastern boundary of Charlecote Park lies the church of St Leonard, built in 1851–3 by John Gibson; it contains the tombs of many of the Lucy family. The tiny village of Charlecote, with some red-brick and timber-framed cottages dating from the seventeenth century, is situated close by.

The Avon valley at Charlecote is level and wide, bounded to the south-east by the ridge of Edge Hill and to the west by the undulating hills north of Stratford-upon-Avon.

As the river flows through the park it receives the waters of a tiny stream, issuing from the lake, and those of the River Dene, or Hele, as Richard Jago referred to it in his poem *Edge-hill*:

Where Avon's Stream, with many a sportive Turn

In addition to the nineteenth-century church of St James, there are the remains of an old Norman church. Inside there is a monument to Nicholas Lane, who died in 1595. Lane sued John Shakespeare, the poet's father, for the non-payment of a debt incurred by his brother Henry, for which he had agreed to act as guarantor. The old church also contains a tablet in memory of William Hirons, a yeoman farmer of Alveston, who was murdered in 1820. He was riding home at night from Warwick when he was attacked by four local men at

Charlecote Mill, dating from the eighteenth century
It was closed in the early 1950s but, after restoration beginning in 1978, it is now working once more, noisily grinding corn. The building is open to the public by appointment and at certain weekends throughout the year. In 1675 the miller, John Dickens, and three others were publicly flogged for 'the felonious stealing and carrying away of two perches and two pikes of the value of 11d'.

Littleham Bridge, near Charlecote. There is a legend that the hollow in which he laid his battered head as he lay dying could never be filled up.

Standing beside the church is the sixteenth-century timber-framed Old Vicarage and across the lane, at the end of a long avenue of limes, is Alveston House, built in 1689. The grounds of the house stretch down to the Avon and, on the Stratford boundary of the estate, the river cascades over the vertical wall of a weir.

The river was made navigable from here to Tewkesbury by William Sandys of Fladbury. Work was completed between 1636 and 1639, but since 1717 the ownership of the river has been separated into two sections: the Upper and Lower Avon, with the dividing line at Evesham.

By the mid nineteenth century the proprietors had ceased to maintain much of the river and parts of it became unnavigable again, particularly the Upper Avon. Restoration began after the Second World War and by 1965 the Lower Avon was re-opened to river traffic.

Work on the Upper Avon followed, and in 1974 HM Queen Elizabeth the Queen Mother officially declared the river open.

In the fifteenth century there were plans to make the Avon navigable from Tewkesbury to Warwick Castle. In the mid 1980s the scheme was revived, but there was considerable opposition from local landowners and nature conservation groups, and the proposal was defeated.

From the weirs at Alveston the river loops around the village, passing the steep wooded banks of Hatton Rock Farm and Ryon Hill, to Tiddington, the site of a small Roman industrial settlement. Excavations in 1925–7 revealed evidence of a flourishing community with corn driers, pottery kilns and smelting furnaces.

In 1938 partial excavations of an Anglo-Saxon cemetery near by unearthed the skeletons of both men and women; the former had been buried with their weapons and the latter with their jewellery. Many of the Roman and Anglo-Saxon artefacts found at Tiddington are on display in the museum at New Place, Stratford-upon-Avon (see p. 103).

Opposite Tiddington there are, in the words of

Charlecote Park and the Avon

The house, its contents and the 228 acres of parkland with its two herds of deer were presented to the National Trust by Sir Montgomerie Fairfax-Lucy in 1946. Although part of the house is still occupied by the present baronet, Sir Edmund Fairfax-Lucy, the rest is open to the public. In addition to the house, the gardens and the park, there is an eighteenth-century brewhouse, a collection of nineteenth-century carriages, a Victorian kitchen and scullery, and a museum of Charlecote history.

William Field, 'a range of proudly swelling mounts, covered for the most part with tufted verdure, adorned with fine trees, some clustered together, others scattered about'. These uplands, now mainly under cultivation, are known as the Welcombe Hills and lie immediately to the north of Stratford-upon-Avon.

On the summit of the hill, above the green golf-links of the Welcombe Hotel, is a 120-feet-high granite obelisk erected in 1876. It stands as a

Near by, the seventeenth-century Clopton House was the home of the Clopton family, who were lords of the manor from the thirteenth to the eighteenth century. The most famous of the Cloptons was Sir Hugh, who went to London and, in 1492, became Lord Mayor. Leland describes how he 'converted a great piece of his substance in good works in Stratford, first making a sumptuous new bridge and large of stone, where in the middle be six great arches for the main stream of Avon, and at each end certain small arches to bear the causey'.

Clopton Bridge, at Stratford, built about 1485, is 366 yards long, with a total of fourteen narrow arches. It replaced 'a poor bridge of timber', which was 'very small and little, and at high waters very hard to pass by', with the result that many 'poor folks . . . stood in jeopardy of life'.

Although the new bridge was much safer than the old one, both ends were washed away by a great flood in 1588, and in 1643, during the English Civil War, part of the bridge was demolished by the Parliamentarians. It was widened in 1814 and a tollhouse added at the Stratford end.

Below Clopton Bridge and the red-brick bridge which once carried the Stratford and Moreton Horse Tramway, the river broadens. On the western bank, beyond the Bancroft Gardens and the Royal Shakespeare Theatre, lies Stratford-upon-Avon – the most famous and most visited market town in England.

memorial to Mark Philips, a Manchester cotton manufacturer, who lived in the Victorian mansion long before it became a hotel.

Welcombe Hills from Snitterfield

The hills are reputed to be the site of a fierce battle between the Britons and the Saxons and, according to Ireland, the extensive entrenchments known as the Dingles 'were thrown up by the soldiers, after their battles, in memory, as well as for cover, of entombing their slain'.

Alveston Weir

This is one of two weirs which link the opposite banks of the river to a small, heavily wooded island around which the Avon temporarily divides. Downstream from here the Avon is navigable all the way to the Severn at Tewkesbury, a distance of over 47 miles. In order to overcome the changes in level of the river, there are a total of seventeen locks, each bypassed by a weir.

CHAPTER 7

STRATFORD-UPON-AVON

*Birthplace Gardens,
Stratford-upon-Avon*
The half-timbered house
originally formed part of a
continuous street frontage, but
the adjoining houses were
demolished in 1857 to reduce
the risk of fire. In the timber-
framed bedroom, with its
uneven ceiling and sloping
floor, the glass in the latticed
window is scored with the
signatures of many
distinguished visitors, including
Sir Walter Scott, Thomas
Carlyle, John Toole, Henry
Irving and Ellen Terry. The
garden has been beautifully laid
out using the trees, plants,
herbs and flowers mentioned in
Shakespeare's works.

Stratford-upon-Avon originated as a river-crossing settlement: Stratford, or the Old English *Stretford*, means 'the ford at which the street crosses the river'. The street, according to Dugdale, referred to 'the great street or road leading from Henley-in-Arden towards London'.

Situated at the intersection of seven main roads, Stratford was from early times a place of some importance. There was a Bronze Age settlement here, a Romano-British village and an Anglo-Saxon monastery.

By 1196 the town had the right to hold a weekly market and in 1214 King John granted it the right to hold a three-day fair. In the sixteenth century William Camden described it as 'a proper little market town' and today there is still a weekly market in Rother Street: 'Rother', in Elizabethan times, meant 'cattle'. The cattle market is now held on a site near the railway station.

The only fair to survive is the annual Mop Fair, held in the streets of the town on 12 October. Traditionally, it was the fair when farm-hands and domestic servants offered their services for hire. Today it is little more than a fun-fair.

In addition to the markets and fairs, which attracted people from the surrounding countryside, the town's development was greatly assisted by the rise of the Guild of the Holy Cross, which fostered crafts and industries.

The guild was founded in the thirteenth century, and until its suppression in 1547 it virtually governed the town. The Guild Chapel was built in about 1269 by Robert de Stratford, but it was almost entirely reconstructed in the fifteenth century. The half-timbered guildhall was erected beside the chapel in 1417–18

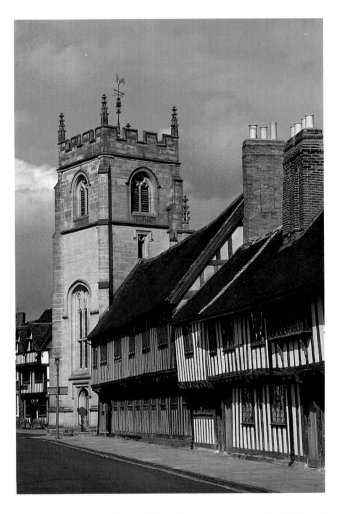

and, at the same time, a number of almshouses were rebuilt for the guild's aged and sick members.

A few years later, a school was founded near by. When the guild was

The Guild Chapel, King Edward VI Grammar School and almshouses, Stratford-upon-Avon
It is generally thought that young Shakespeare attended the school and not only received a classical education but also, in the hall below, saw plays performed by travelling actors. The half-timbered almshouses adjoining the guildhall still house the elderly.

suppressed, only the school was allowed to continue. It was transferred to the upper floor of the guildhall and the classes held in a large room, now known as 'Big School', which is used today by the King Edward VI Grammar School.

In 1553 Stratford was granted a charter of incorporation by King Edward VI and became entitled to elect its own officers with self-governing powers. The minute books of the early corporate body, preserved in the archives of the Shakespeare Birthplace Trust, reveal that Shakespeare's father, John, held various offices and became bailiff, or mayor, in 1568.

John Shakespeare was a yeoman farmer of Snitterfield, a small village a few miles north of Stratford. By 1551 he had moved to Stratford and established himself as a glover and dealer in wool. Six years later he married Mary Arden, one of eight daughters of Robert Arden, a wealthy yeoman farmer, who lived at Wilmcote, three miles north-west of the busy market town.

It is documented that John and Mary Shakespeare owned and occupied premises in Henley Street, Stratford-upon-Avon, as early as 1552. Their house, now known as the Birthplace, originally formed part of a continuous street frontage. At the time of William's birth, in April 1564, the property consisted of two separate buildings: the Shakespeare family home and their shop and warehouse.

Although there is no record of when the first 'tourists' began to visit the Birthplace, it is known that the house figured prominently in the Stratford Jubilee of 1769, organized by the actor David Garrick, 'in honour and to the memory of Shakespeare'.

Garrick's Jubilee marked the beginning of a new era for the town. From then on the number of people visiting the Birthplace each year gradually increased and today the figure is climbing steadily towards the million mark.

In 1582, at the age of eighteen, William Shakespeare married Anne Hathaway, the daughter of Richard Hathaway, a yeoman farmer of Shottery, a small hamlet a mile to the west of Stratford. The Hathaway family lived in a spacious twelve-roomed farmhouse, originally called Hewlands Farm but now

Mary Arden's House, Wilmcote

Mary Arden was the mother of William Shakespeare. This timber-framed farmstead, its roof covered with clay tiles and its foundations built with local blue-grey stone, dates from the early sixteenth century. It was occupied as a farmhouse until 1930, when it was acquired by The Shakespeare Birthplace Trust. The barns and outbuildings at the rear of the house contain a fascinating collection of old agricultural implements, domestic utensils, craftsmen's tools, farm carts and wagons and an old cider press.

known as Anne Hathaway's Cottage. The oldest part of the half-timbered building, with its high-pitched thatched roof, tall brick chimney-stacks and tiny latticed windows, dates back to the fifteenth century. It was owned and occupied by the Hathaways until 1892, when it was purchased by the Trustees and Guardians of Shakespeare's Birthplace. The old-fashioned garden contains a host of traditional flowers, including 'bold oxlips', crown imperials, foxgloves, hollyhocks, 'nodding' violets, 'pale primroses', columbines and 'morning roses newly washed with dew'.

On 26 May 1583, according to the Stratford parish register, Anne and William's first child, Susanna, was baptized. Two years later, they had twins, Hamnet and Judith. Shortly afterwards, Shakespeare left Stratford.

Anne Hathaway's Cottage, Shottery

Anne Hathaway married William Shakespeare in 1582. In spring and summer, her family home attracts parties from all over the world, with one coach after another depositing their camera-clicking passengers at the garden gate. But in winter, when icicles hang from the thatch and snow lies thick upon the ground and the resident robin fluffs its feathers against the cold, visitors are few and far between.

From 1592, at the age of twenty-eight, he can be traced in London, first as an actor and then as a reviser of plays. He became a writer and part-owner of the Globe Theatre, built on the southern bank of the Thames in 1599. The publication of *Venus and Adonis* in 1593 was followed by a prodigious stream of poems and plays and, within a few years, he had become a wealthy and successful man.

However, Shakespeare did not forget Stratford, for in 1597, a year after the death of his son, Hamnet, he purchased New Place, one of the largest houses in the town. Once owned by Sir Hugh Clopton, it stood beside the medieval Guild Chapel and the grammar school. The grounds were extensive, with barns, a mulberry tree, cultivated gardens and two orchards that stretched

down to the River Avon. It was described by Leland in 1540 as 'a pretty house of brick and timber', but today only the foundations remain.

The site of New Place eventually became the garden of the house next door

Nash's House and New Place Museum, Stratford-upon-Avon

New Place was purchased by Shakespeare in 1597 for £60. In 1610 he settled here permanently and, reputedly after drinking with Ben Jonson and Michael Drayton, he died in the house on 23 April 1616. In 1759, however, the property was pulled down by the bad-tempered owner, the Revd Francis Gastrell, who was subsequently driven out of the town by the enraged inhabitants. Nash's House, next door to New Place, was the home of Elizabeth Hall, Shakespeare's granddaughter, who married Thomas Nash in 1626. It now contains a museum of local history.

(Nash's House) and in 1862 the entire property was acquired by the Trustees of what is now the Shakespeare Birthplace Trust. Beyond the turf-covered foundations there is a replica of an Elizabethan knot-garden, modelled on the intricate designs of the period.

Shakespeare's daughter Susanna became the wife of one of the town's leading physicians, Dr John Hall, in 1607 and lived at Hall's Croft in Old Town, near by. It is not known whether Shakespeare was ever treated by Dr Hall, but after his retirement to New Place in about 1610 he would have been a frequent visitor to Hall's Croft.

William Shakespeare died on 23 April 1616, his fifty-second birthday. Two days later, he was buried in the chancel of Holy Trinity Church on the banks of the Avon. Buried near by are his wife, his daughter Susanna, her husband Dr John Hall and Thomas Nash, the husband of Shakespeare's granddaughter.

Sir Walter Scott came with his sister to view the poet's grave in April 1828 and wrote in his journal: 'We visited the tomb of the mighty wizzard. It is in the bad taste of James I's reign; but what a magic does the locality possess!'

Each year on St George's Day, England's Day and the day of Shakespeare's birth and death, his grave is overwhelmed by a mountain of floral tributes from over a hundred countries.

As Ben Jonson, the 'mighty wizzard's' friend and contemporary, said of him,

> Thou art a monument, without a tomb,
> And art alive still, while thy book doth live,
> And we have wits to read, and praise to give.

A short distance upstream from Holy Trinity Church stands the Royal Shakespeare Theatre. The Swan Theatre adjoining it was the gift of an anonymous benefactor and was officially opened by Queen Elizabeth II in November 1986.

Holy Trinity Church, Stratford-upon-Avon, in which Shakespeare was buried

Inscribed on the stone that marks his grave there is a curse, said to have been written by himself:

Good Frend for Jesus Sake
   Forbeare
To Digg the Dust Encloased
   Heare.
Blest Be ye Man yt Spares thes
   Stones
And Curst be He yt Moves
   My Bones.

In the Bancroft Gardens, in front of the main theatre, is a bronze statue of Shakespeare mounted on a high pedestal and surrounded by four characters from his plays: Lady Macbeth, Hamlet, Prince Hal and Falstaff, symbolizing

Hall's Croft and garden,
Old Town,
Stratford-upon-Avon
The half-timbered, many-
gabled house was the home of
Shakespeare's daughter
Susanna and her husband Dr
John Hall. It is one of the
finest surviving Elizabethan
buildings in Stratford.

respectively tragedy, philosophy, history and comedy.

Below the seated poet, and within the Bancroft Gardens, lies the Stratford Canal Basin, where those visiting the town by boat can moor overnight. The twenty-five-mile Stratford-upon-Avon Canal, connecting with the Worcester and Birmingham Canal at King's Norton (and joining the Grand Union Canal at Lapworth), is joined to the Avon by means of a wide lock, restored in 1963.

Mary Mackay, who lived at Mason Croft for twenty years until her death in 1924 and wrote novels under the name of Marie Corelli, had herself transported up and down the Avon in a full-size gondola imported from Venice. But after frequent complaints about her gondolier's lack of competence and a drunken argument in which he pulled out a knife, he was dismissed.

STRATFORD-UPON-AVON TO EVESHAM

Downstream from the theatre and the church, the Avon divides; two branches tumble over weirs (one stepped and the other sloping) while the third passes through the deep Colin P. Witter Lock, formerly Stratford New Lock. Many locks on the Upper Avon, including this one, were built with the help of volunteers from English gaols. It was opened on 1 June 1974 by Queen Elizabeth II.

Opposite the lock is the new Avonside housing development. Near by is a tall block of ugly but 'very desirable apartments', built in 1974 on the site of Lucy's Mill.

The Avon, passing under the Mill Footbridge and the disused bridge which once carried the Stratford and Midland Junction Railway, heads south-westwards, into flat and peaceful countryside. A short distance downstream, beyond a few narrow islands, the river enters Weir Brake Lock or Anonymous Lock, as it is also called, in honour of the anonymous donors who supported the Upper Avon Navigation Trust's restoration fund. It was the last lock to be completed on the waterway.

Trees are everywhere, crack willows particularly, their gnarled trunks hosting wild blackberries, sweet honeysuckle and the briars of dog roses. Throughout the summer breeding period, swallows and house martins swoop over the river, catching insects to feed their young.

Beyond the bridge carrying the disused Great Western Railway Stratford-to-Cheltenham line, the Avon is joined by the River Stour, which rises in the Cotswold hills.

In his topographical poem *Poly-Olbion*, Michael Drayton, born at Hartshill, Warwickshire, in 1563, sums up the Avon's winding journey from Warwick where it

entertains the high complexioned Leam:
And as she thence along to Stratford on doth strain,
Receiveth little Hele the next into her train:
Then taketh in the Stour, the brook, of all the rest
Which that most goodly Vale of Red-horse loveth best.

It is thought that much of the long poem was written at Clifford Chambers, situated about one mile upstream of the Stour's confluence with the Avon. The seventeenth-century manor-house was restored by Sir Edwin Lutyens after being severely damaged by a fire in 1918.

There is a tradition that Shakespeare was born in

Hillborough Manor with its circular stone dovecote
There is a tradition that Charles II, after his escape from the battle of Worcester in 1651, came to Hillborough and left his treasure at the manor-house before fleeing across the river to Long Marston.

the village when his mother came to the rectory to escape from the Stratford plague of 1564. The claim is, of course, disputed by the citizens of Stratford-upon-Avon.

On the west bank of the river, opposite the Milcote Sewage Disposal Works, the village of Luddington lies strung out along its one long road, with many of the gardens running down to the water's edge. It consists of a variety of old and modern houses, including a number of attractive sixteenth- and seventeenth-century cottages (some thatched), farmsteads and a church rebuilt in 1872.

Many of the villages in the vicinity of Stratford-upon-Avon lay claim to associations with Shakespeare. Luddington is no exception. There is a strong tradition that William and Anne were married in Luddington church. Unfortunately, the original building was destroyed by fire and the church registers were lost.

At the western end of the village, below Luddington Lock, is the Ministry of Agriculture, Fisheries and Food's Experimental Horticulture Station with orchards sweeping down towards the Avon.

On the other side of the river, its squat embattled tower peeping above the trees, is the tiny church of All Saints, Weston-on-Avon. The hamlet lies in a cul-de-sac and contains some charming houses and cottages, but has no shop, no public house, no post office and no school.

The Royal Shakespeare Theatre, Stratford-upon-Avon
The current building was completed in 1932 after the original theatre was destroyed by fire in 1926.

Welford-on-Avon, its considerably larger neighbour, is said to have had a maypole on the village green since the sixteenth century. The pole, over seventy feet high, with a weather-vane on the top, is spirally painted red, white and blue and has been skipped and danced around by children from the village school for generations.

The village, which has been engulfed by extensive housing developments, still contains some black and white timber-framed thatched cottages, the prettiest row standing near the church in Boat Lane. The lane – and Mill Lane, which runs parallel to it – leads down to the river where there is a weir and the W. A. Cadbury Lock, built in 1971 with the help of volunteers from Gloucester Gaol. The remains of the old lock lie buried on the island between the new lock and the weir.

Close by is the site of one of the two mills which were in existence in 1291. The mill near the lock was working until 1958 and has now been converted into a private residence. The church of St Peter, the oldest parts dating from the twelfth century, was restored in 1867 by Sir George Gilbert Scott.

North of Welford-on-Avon, where the road from Binton to Long Marston crosses the river, is a public house called The Four Alls. It is said to take its name from 'A king who rules over all; a parson who prays for all; a soldier who fights for all; and a farmer who pays for all.'

Binton Bridges, close by, is a succession of twelve stone arches, forming a number of bridges which span the Avon by means of two small islands.

Binton belonged to the monastery of Evesham early in the eighth century. The church of St Peter, surrounded by trees, was rebuilt in 1876 and contains a stained-glass memorial window to Captain Robert F. Scott, who died after reaching the South Pole in 1912.

Continuing its journey downstream from Binton Bridges, the Avon loops around Welford-on-Avon and, flowing past Cadbury Lock and the ruins of Lower Welford Lock, heads towards Bidford-on-Avon.

On the hillside north of Pilgrim Lock, which was built from thousands of concrete blocks, is Hill-

borough, and probably the site of a lost village. It is said that a ghostly woman in white and a spectral stag haunt one of the surrounding fields.

The hamlet, situated at the end of a long lane, consists of a sixteenth-century manor-house, a farmhouse, a few dwellings and a circular dovecote with room for 900 pigeons. There was a chapel dedicated to St Mary Magdalene but it was demolished in the sixteenth century.

Half a mile downstream, near where it is joined by the Dorsington Brook, the Avon is split by a large island. Alongside it stands Bidford Grange, formerly the grange of Bordesley Abbey.

South of the Grange the land is flat and low-lying and, when the river floods its banks, the Welford Road is usually impassable.

Colin P. Witter Lock,
Stratford-upon-Avon

Barton, standing on higher ground directly south of the Elsie and Hiram Billington Lock, is a small hamlet with a large two-storeyed manor-house dated 1663. In addition to a number of sixteenth- and seventeenth-century timber-framed buildings (some thatched) there is an inn called The Cottage of Content.

On the outskirts of the hamlet, sprawling along the river bank, is a caravan site and, a short distance upstream, a boat-hire company.

From here the Avon flows through open fields and meadows to Bidford-on-Avon, where it is crossed by an eight-arched stone bridge. The village stands on an old Roman road, known as Ryknild Street to the north and Buckle Street to the south.

It consists of a single street with the earliest buildings standing near the church and the river. The largest, the former Falcon Inn, now a private residence, dates from the sixteenth century and is built of local lias stone. It stands opposite the churchyard, on a corner of the High Street and near the old market square.

Bidford-on-Avon is one of the so-called Shakespeare villages and there is a tradition that the poet (together with Michael Drayton and Ben Jonson or with a group of locals) engaged in a drinking bout at the Falcon Inn against the so-called 'Bidford Topers'. The legend was first published in 1762 in an anonymous letter printed in *The British Magazine, or Monthly Repository for Gentlemen and Ladies.*

Thirty years later, on his journey down the Avon, Ireland also relates the story, which refers to a large crab-apple tree, under which the drunken 'Stratford lads' encamped for the night 'in a very disorderly and unmilitary form'.

The apple tree, known as Shakespeare's Crab, was still standing by the side of the Stratford Road in 1820 when Washington Irving published the story in *The Sketch Book.* It was cut down in 1824 and by the end of the century a new one had been planted.

Leaving Bidford-on-Avon, the river passes Big Meadow, a twenty-six-acre recreation area popular with residents and day-trippers, and curves south through rich farmland to Marlcliff.

As the Avon enters the Vale of Evesham the landscape gradually alters: the arable fields give way to orchards, fruit farms and market gardens. Within the space of about five miles the change is almost total.

At Marlcliff the river is deflected westwards by a wall of very hard marl clay, which made the task of constructing the nearby lock almost impossible.

The lock, called the Inland Waterways Association Lock, was built in 1969, with enormous effort

and expense, by the Royal Engineers, men from Gloucester Gaol and other volunteers. In addition to blasting out a navigation channel through the solid Marlcliff slab, the weir had to be raised to increase the river level.

The cliff rises abruptly to a height of over one hundred feet above the river; clinging to its precipitous slopes is a mass of trees and bushes, many overhung with dog roses and traveller's joy.

The hamlet of Marlcliff consists of two stone farmhouses, a number of stone or timber-framed cottages, all dating from the seventeenth century, and some modern houses. Many of the cottages have beautifully kept gardens.

The nine-mile footpath following the Avon from Marlcliff to Stratford-upon-Avon was opened on 27 June 1987 by the Chairman of the Ramblers' Association.

The footpath downstream to Cleeve Prior passes through meadows and fields full of bird, animal and insect life. Between Marlcliff and the confluence of the Avon and the Arrow the Avon forms the boundary of Warwickshire and Hereford and Worcester.

It is said that, at least two centuries ago, the original confluence of the rivers was about half a mile downstream at Cleeve Mill and that the present junction was formed by an artificial cut.

The Arrow rises on the hills above Alvechurch, flows through Redditch and Alcester and passes

Bidford-on-Avon bridge and the church of St Lawrence
The bridge was built in the fifteenth century to replace an ancient ford situated near the church. It was erected two hundred yards downstream; the diversion of the road may account for the lopsided layout of the village.

Ragley Hall, the seventeenth-century home of the Marquess and Marchioness of Hertford. A short distance downstream, near where it joins the Avon in Worcester Meadows, is Salford Priors.

The village takes its name from a nearby ford on the old Salt Way from Droitwich to Hillborough. In 708 the manor was given to Evesham Abbey by Kenred, King of Mercia, and, during the reign of Edward the Confessor, was held by Lady Godiva, the wife of Leofric, Earl of Coventry. In 1122 Geoffrey de Clinton granted it to Kenilworth Priory, from which it derived the name of Salford Priors.

In fact there were two Salfords: Salford Minor, lying less than a mile to the south-west of Salford Major, remained in the possession of the Abbot of

Tenpenny Cottage, Welford-upon-Avon

Evesham until the Dissolution and consequently became known as Abbot's Salford.

Although Salford Priors consists largely of modern houses, a few sixteenth- or seventeenth-century timber-framed thatched cottages remain. The church of St Matthew, restored in 1874, was originally Norman and has a fourteenth-century turret which, it has been suggested, may have been a beacon to guide travellers crossing the ford.

Salford Hall, standing on the opposite side of the road from Stratford-upon-Avon to Evesham, dates from the fifteenth century. The original house was built by the Abbots of Evesham and was once thought to contain a chapel. It was enlarged in 1602 using a variety of stone: local blue lias, sandstone and Cotswold oolite limestone. Between 1807 and 1838 it was occupied by a community of English Benedictine nuns from Cambrai and is still locally called the Nunnery. It is now a hotel.

The low-lying land to the west of the Salfords was extremely marshy until it was drained in the early nineteenth century. Rising steeply from the Avon's flood plain is the long, tree-covered escarpment of Cleeve Hill, almost one hundred feet high. It was once an important source of building limestone and traces of the abandoned and now-overgrown pits and quarries remain.

At the foot of the cliff, or cleeve, at least until the period between the two world wars, there was a mill, a weir and a footbridge, linking Salford Priors

The Avon at Marlcliff
Prior to 1860 and the introduction of steam tugs, barges on the Avon, which was without tow-paths, were pulled by gangs of 'bow haulers'. 'The navigation is conducted in a primitive fashion,' wrote Thorne in 1845. 'Horses were not employed to draw the barges at first, nor are they now. At a huge heavy laden craft five or six strong men may be seen tugging laboriously; a miserable service for human beings to be put to . . .'

to Cleeve Prior. All have been demolished: the mill during the early 1940s and the weir during the restoration of the waterway in the late sixties and early seventies. In order to produce a navigation channel the ford, across which the army of Prince Edward (the son of Henry III) waded in 1265 – see p. 124 – was also dredged away.

At the top of the road, on the summit of the wooded cliff, is a nature reserve opened by Lord Melchett on 17 October 1983 on behalf of the Worcestershire Nature Conservation Trust. Beneath the footpath running the whole length of the ridge and overlooking the Avon valley lies an ancient Roman road.

The village of Cleeve Prior is situated at the northern end of the reserve and, although it has

Stubble burning

In late summer, after the grain has been harvested, the remaining stubble is often burnt to remove weeds and their seeds in readiness for the next crop.

een enlarged by modern houses and bungalows, he oldest buildings belong more to the Cotswolds han to the Avon valley. Most of the houses and ottages around the triangular village green are built f local oolite limestone, as are also the Jacobean manor-house, the King's Arms inn and the church of St Andrew.

The Warwickshire and Hereford and Worcester county boundary runs down the centre of the Avon, from the sprawling riverside caravan site

Middle Littleton tithe barn
The 140 ft long barn was built in the thirteenth or fourteenth century by the Abbots of Evesham and was given to the National Trust in 1975.

near the ruins of Cleeve Mill for just over a mile before turning acutely north between Abbot's Salford and Harvington.

Once in Hereford and Worcester the river's windings become more marked and it takes over thirty-one miles to cross the south-east of the county, a distance of fifteen miles.

After hugging the foot of Cleeve Hill for three quarters of a mile the river suddenly sweeps away from the ridge into fertile meadows full of cattle and sheep. Rising from the broad and level plain beyond the distant towers and spires of Evesham is 'the huge gloomy mass' of Bredon Hill.

Near the site of the old Upper Harvington Lock is the Robert Aickman New Lock, built in 1982 to replace the earlier Aickman Lock which had been the first to be built by the Upper Avon Navigation Trust. Aickman founded the Inland Waterways Association in 1946 and was an influential figure in the restoration of the Upper Avon navigation.

From the derelict remains of Harvington Mill a footpath leads across the meadows to the village of Harvington, which contains a few pleasant black and white cottages and a Norman church restored in the nineteenth century. The former railway station, which used to be on the old Birmingham-to-Evesham line, is now the headquarters of the Upper Avon Navigation Trust.

Half a mile downstream the river takes a right-angled turn to the west and on the corner is the Fish and Anchor Inn and a weir, often used by white-water canoeists.

In 1906 Garrett found his boat journey upstream, described in *The Idyllic Avon*, hindered by shallows and obstructed not only by a 'decayed lock and weir' but also by a ford. 'After some amount of hauling we succeed in getting our boat over the ford at the Fish and Anchor. Above the ford the banks of the river are rather high, especially near the inn, and the ferry-boat there is approached by a curious little flight of steps.' The ferry, which ceased operation for almost fifty years, has recently been re-established, though not to its former glory – the 'new' ferry is a hand-winched, floating rubbish skip!

A new lock was built in 1969 a short distance downstream from the ford and weir and called the George Billington Lock, after the man who gave his life-savings of £5,000 to fund its construction. A cylindrical lock-keeper's tower was added in 1981.

The new canal, cut through Anchor Meadow, is spanned by a twelve-ton bridge and on it there is a plaque which reads: 'In memory of William Smith of Evesham, 1830–1906, who fought hard for the restoration of the Upper Avon'.

To the east of the Fish and Anchor Inn, standing on a hill, are the villages of North Littleton, Middle Littleton and South Littleton. North and Middle Littleton, however, have merged over the centuries to become one large village. Near the ancient church of St Nicholas in Middle Littleton is a beautiful seventeenth-century stone manor-house and, standing behind it, an enormous tithe barn.

The church of St Nicholas and the neighbouring church of St Michael at South Littleton are both adorned with a gruesome collection of gargoyles.

On the opposite side of the valley, surrounded by orchards, is Norton. Its parish church is dedicated to St Egwin, the founder of Evesham Abbey. The land at nearby Lenchwick was cleared and brought

into cultivation by Abbot Randolph, who constructed a grange and a fish-pond there early in the thirteenth century. The site of the latter can still be located.

From Norton Corner and the island known as Cox's Bottom, the Avon turns sharply south and, with orchards sloping down to the water's edge, arrives at the Bridge Inn, Offenham, the site of a former ferry.

The bridge, which has long disappeared without trace, was described by Leland in about 1540 as 'a narrow stone bridge for footmen'. But in 1795 Ireland said that 'no traces of it appear'. It may have been removed and the ferry instituted in its place in 1637, when the river was made navigable.

Almost opposite the inn is a partial island, known as Dead Men's Ait, on which many Welsh soldiers were massacred after the battle of Evesham in 1265 (see p. 125). A large quantity of human remains was discovered here in the eighteenth century.

The village of Offenham is said to have taken its name from Offa, King of Mercia, to whom it belonged in the ninth century. He gave part of it to the monks of Evesham Abbey and they later obtained the rest. The manor-house, to which the last abbot, Clement Lichfield, retired after the Dissolution, no longer survives, although its moat can still be discerned near Manor Farm.

The village is large and, with its modern housing developments and improvements, has suffered the

Timber-framed house, Offenham

fate of many of the villages around Evesham. Near the church of St Mary and St Milburga, restored in 1862, is a tall, brightly coloured maypole similar to the one at Welford-on-Avon. In spring it is fes-tooned with ribbons and bunting and on May Day mornings it is said to be impossible to sleep because of the festivities. A plaque states that 'A maypole is known to have been here since 1860. This new pole was prepared over three years and erected by the Wake Committee 27 September 1987.'

In the vicinity of Church Street and Gibbs Lane there are a few attractive stone and timber-framed cottages, some thatched and others tiled.

Below the riverside Bridge Inn at Offenham the Avon is joined by a small stream which Ireland refers to as the 'Fork' and Showell as the 'Falke'. It is formed by a number of streams which rise on the Cotswold hills, including the Badsey Brook from world-famous Broadway.

The land is now almost entirely devoted to market gardening and fruit growing. The fields that are not concealed by fruit trees lie hidden beneath a sea of shining glass, where peas, beans, lettuces, radishes, tomatoes, strawberries, spring onions, cabbage, asparagus and many more thrive in the warm light soil of the Vale. In spring, when the plum, apple and pear trees are in flower, visitors are attracted like bees to the blossom. But un-fortunately the beauty of the scene is marred by rows of electricity pylons with heavy overhead power lines slung between them.

The Avon flows south from Offenham and within a couple of miles doubles back on itself to

Apples in an orchard, Vale of Evesham

form a U; originally confined within the peninsula was the old town of Evesham, an important market centre for the produce of the Vale.

CHAPTER 8

EVESHAM

In about the year AD 700 Egwin, Bishop of Worcester, acted over-zealously in trying to convert the pagan worshippers in his diocese to Christianity. He made himself so unpopular that the local inhabitants hauled him before Ethelred, King of Mercia. The matter was referred to Rome and the Pope commanded Egwin to appear before him to answer the charges.

As an act of humility Egwin fastened a pair of iron horse-fetters to his ankles, locked them and threw the key into the Avon. Securely shackled, he journeyed to Rome to proclaim his innocence. On his arrival a miracle is said to have occurred. One of his attendants, while fishing in the Tiber, hooked a salmon. The fish leapt obediently on to the bank and landed itself. When it was cut open the key to the bishop's fetters was found in its stomach. The Pope took this event as a sign of Egwin's innocence and the charges were immediately dismissed.

On Egwin's triumphant return King Ethelred restored him to his see. He also gave Egwin a large tract of wild land almost impossible to cultivate.

Egwin, however, kept pigs and he let them forage on it. He divided the land into four sections and appointed a swine-herd to look after each. Eoves was given charge of the eastern portion.

One day a sow wandered off into the undergrowth and in his attempts to find it Eoves became lost. When at last he stumbled upon the missing beast she had given birth to three piglets. The sow grunted and trotted off into the forest with its young. Eoves followed them into an open glade where, to his astonishment,

The Almonry Museum from the south, Evesham
The part-stone, part-timber-framed building, which is also a tourist information centre, is considered to be the finest example of early domestic architecture in the town. Dating from the fourteenth or fifteenth century, it stands on or near the site of the old monastic almonry, the home of the abbey almoner, whose duty was to administer charity to the sick and the poor.

he beheld a wondrous vision of the Virgin Mary accompanied by two angels singing celestial songs.

On Eoves's escape from the wilderness, he reported his experience to Egwin, who wanted to see the place for himself. Eoves led the bishop to the glade and the vision reappeared to instruct Egwin to build an abbey upon the site. The monastery, and the subsequent town that arose because of the miraculous vision, was named 'Eovesholme' or Evesham.

The Benedictine monastery became one of the most powerful abbeys in England. When Egwin died in 717, he was buried in the abbey church and his shrine became a place of international pilgrimage.

The original church collapsed in about 960 and was rebuilt in the eleventh century. The only section to survive the Dissolution intact was the bell tower.

One of the entrances to the abbey is Abbot Reginald's Gateway, built in the twelfth century and situated at the southern end of Market Place. The timber-framed buildings over and adjacent to it were probably erected in the fifteenth century. Within the abbey wall there are two parish churches: the church of All Saints and the church of St Lawrence. Many items and relics once belonging to the abbey are now preserved in the Almonry Museum, owned by Evesham Town Council and managed by the Vale of Evesham Historical Society.

In the rear garden of the Almonry is a stone cross dredged from the Avon at Pershore Old Bridge in 1955.

The museum's de Montfort Room, opened in 1965 to commemorate the 700th anniversary of the battle of Evesham, contains plans, photographs, documents and relics illustrating the life of Simon de Montfort and the battle in which he died.

The de Montforts, Norman in origin, were one of the great families of medieval Warwickshire. Simon married the youngest sister of Henry III, Eleanor, in 1238. At first he and the king were friends.

Henry, however, repeatedly broke his promises to abide by the terms of Magna Carta which his father, King John, had signed in 1215. Eventually the

Church of St Lawrence, Evesham
It is thought that the church was built exclusively for pilgrims in order to enable the townsfolk to worship in All Saints without the risk of catching any contagious diseases.

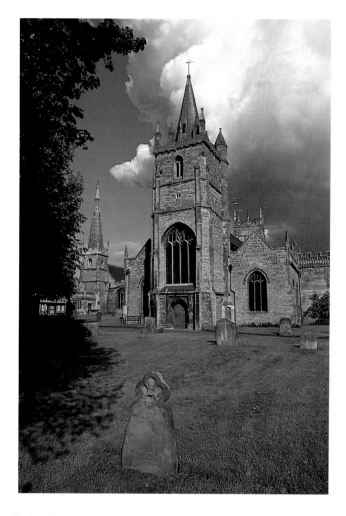

barons rebelled. Simon, appointed as their leader, initiated a programme of reform that would give power to an elected council of representatives. It was a revolutionary programme which led, inevitably, to war.

In 1264 Henry was defeated and captured, with his son, Prince Edward, in the battle of Lewes, Sussex. The following year Simon's army was heading towards the Severn, taking the king and his son with them as hostages, when Prince Edward managed to escape.

Edward set up a royalist headquarters at Worcester and gathered together a powerful army. Anticipating that de Montfort would try to make for Kenilworth to join the army of his son, Simon, Edward sent part of his army to Kenilworth and managed to disperse the younger Simon's force.

At Worcester, on 3 August 1265, Edward learned that de Montfort's army had crossed the Severn. He decided to march towards Evesham to block the elder Simon's passage north.

When de Montfort and the barons entered Evesham that evening, to be welcomed by the Abbey, they were unaware of the trap they were marching into. Edward dispersed his forces to cover de Montfort's every means of escape. Enclosed on three sides by the Avon and with the ten-thousand-strong army of Prince Edward to the north, de Montfort had to attack. Outnumbered roughly two to one, he tried to smash his way through the royalist line.

Simon de Montfort was slain in the massacre that followed. 'Such was the murder of Evesham,' wrote Robert of Gloucester, 'for battle it was none.' According to the chroniclers, when he died the sky grew black as the sound of thunder and huge bolts of lightning shook the earth.

The mutilated remains of de Montfort were buried in the abbey church. Evesham, however, had a long-established reputation for its healing shrines and the tomb of the earl proved to be no exception: 'The people conceived an opinion, that this Earl being slain, fighting in defence of the liberties of the realm, and performance of his oath as they took it, died a martyr: which by the bruited holiness of his past life and miracles ascribed to him after his death, was greatly confirmed in the next age.'

The veneration shown to de Montfort's grave and the numerous miracles that were reported forced Henry to exhume the body and bury it in a secret place. It did no good. It seems that Simon de Montfort was

> *chosen from above,*
> *By inspiration of celestial grace,*
> *To work exceeding miracles on earth.*
>
> 1 Henry VI

Hundreds of miracles were recorded over the following years. The waters of the spring near where Simon was killed became famed for their healing properties. Evesham became a great pilgrimage centre. Lured by reports of miraculous cures, the sick travelled in their thousands from all over Europe to worship at the sacred shrines.

EVESHAM TO PERSHORE

Evesham Lock, just over a mile downstream from Offenham, marks the boundary between the Upper and Lower Avon, though historically the division is marked by Workman Bridge. In 1717 the lock was defined as belonging to the Upper Avon but in 1964 the Lower Avon Navigation Trust was responsible for rebuilding it.

No craft may pass through the lock without a valid licence which can be obtained from the Lock House, an A-frame dwelling built in 1972; it spans a water channel that once housed an eel trap. The old brick mill near by is now used as a social club.

To the north of the lock there are moorings, boatyards, slipways, a marina and the buildings of Evesham Sailing Club.

A short distance downstream is Workman Bridge, dedicated 'to the public spirit and perseverance of Henry Workman Esq.' and opened in 1856. It replaced the medieval bridge of eight arches and links Evesham with the village of Bengeworth.

In the twelfth century there was a castle at Bengeworth, belonging to William de Beauchamp, who was accused of robbing the church and destroying the cemetery walls. The Abbot of Evesham Abbey, William de Anderville, therefore excommunicated him and, having gained possession of the castle, set about pulling it down. After this, the site became a burial ground.

The main road from Evesham through Bengeworth leads to the Cotswold village of Broadway. Midway between them is Wickhamford, noted for its connection with George Washington, a collateral descendant from the family of Penelope Washington, who once lived in Wickhamford Manor. She died in 1697 and on her tomb is the Washington coat of arms, the stars and stripes, on which the national flag of the United States of America was based.

From the old port of Bengeworth the banks of the Avon, now a substantial river, are flanked by magnificent trees. Sweeping down to the water's edge are the lawns of Abbey Park and near the site of the old abbey's high altar stands a memorial stone to Simon de Montfort.

The abbey's lavishly adorned bell tower, 110 feet high, dominates the park, while beyond stand the two parish churches of All Saints and St Lawrence. A short distance downstream are the buildings of the Evesham Rowing Club.

On the opposite bank, running along Waterside,

are the Workman Gardens, with moorings near by. Public gardens and recreation areas stretch alongside the river to Evesham New Bridge. A few hundred yards downstream from the bridge the Avon is joined by the little River Isbourne.

At the south-western extremity of the Avon's huge loop around Evesham lies Hampton, now practically a suburb of the market town. Although Hampton is heavily built up, with modern houses and an industrial estate, the church of St Andrew, built in Perpendicular style, is very attractive. Unusually for this part of England, it has a central tower.

Below the ferry at Hampton, Clark's Hill, covered with orchards, 'verges upon the river for near a mile'. Having almost circled Evesham the river now straightens out and heads north. The battle of 1265 took place on the summit of the heavily wooded hill ahead. Near the top, in the grounds of Abbey Manor, stands an obelisk commemorating the battle. Near by, almost hidden by the trees, is another memorial, known as Leicester's Tower.

At the foot of the hill the Avon turns sharply north-west. On the north bank are the boatyard and slipway of Sankey Marine, where limited moorings are available.

About half a mile downstream is Chadbury Lock, which is partially obscured by trees. Near the lock and the weir is a converted mill. The village lies to the north of it and, according to its name, was once a fortification belonging to Chad, a seventh-century bishop of Mercia.

North-west of Chadbury is the BBC Engineering Training Centre at Wood Norton. The house, standing on high ground and surrounded by woodland, was formerly the seat of the Duc d'Aumale and then his great-nephew the Duc d'Orléans, pretender to the throne of France. It was also used by King Manuel after his deposition from the throne of Portugal in 1910.

After leaving Evesham the river winds and twists around the base of Bredon Hill. As the Avon weaves past Wood Norton towards Pershore, the hill begins to impress itself on the landscape and, within ten miles, it dominates the scene entirely.

Across the river from Wood Norton is Charlton. A small stream, called the Merry Brook, rises on the slopes of Bredon Hill and flows through the centre of the village's large green, around which are a number of old black and white thatched cottages.

The Dingley or Dineley family were lords of the Manor of Charlton from the fourteenth to the close of the eighteenth century, when the line came to an end. Henry Workman was the lord of Charlton manor in the mid nineteenth century and during his

ownership of the estate the medieval tithe barn was converted into a church.

Craycombe Hill, to the north of Charlton, is mainly covered with mixed woodland and orchards. On its southern slope, hidden from the river by trees, is Craycombe House, built in the late eighteenth century.

Francis Brett Young, the novelist, poet and physician, lived in the house for a few years. In *The Island*, written between 1940 and 1944, he describes the Avon from its source to its confluence with the Severn.

The village of Fladbury lies on the west bank of the Avon and archaeological excavations indicate that there was a Bronze Age settlement here in about 2000 BC. There was a monastery at Fladbury in AD 691 when Ethelred, King of Mercia, granted the territory which is called Fledanburg' to Oftfor, Bishop of Worcester.

The mill belonging to the bishop was valued at ten shillings a year with an annual rent of 500 eels. Fladbury Mill, dating from the sixteenth century, is situated on the western side of the weir opposite Cropthorne Mill, built about 1700. Both are now private residences.

The church of St John the Baptist, restored in 1865 and 1871, contains the tomb of Sir John Throckmorton, who died in 1445, and a monument to George Perrott, the builder of Craycombe House, who died in 1806.

The village of Fladbury, containing a mixture of old and modern properties, is very attractive, especially along the riverside, where the gardens of the houses are adorned with some magnificent trees. Red-brick mills, broad foaming weirs, steep crumbling banks and rich dark foliage, contrast with the meadows beyond. It is a favourite spot for fishermen.

Linking Fladbury with the neighbouring villages of Charlton and Cropthorne is the Jubilee Bridge, erected in 1933. It replaced an earlier bridge, built to mark the 1887 Jubilee of Queen Victoria. Prior to that there used to be a ford.

Cropthorne lies on high ground nearly a mile downstream from Fladbury. The main street runs parallel to the waterway and many of the gardens slope down to the Avon's edge. Among the modern houses there are still some delightful black and white, timber-framed thatched cottages. The church of St Michael dates from the twelfth century and contains a number of monuments to the Dingley family, to whom the manor formerly belonged.

Inside the church, mounted on a stone block, is a ninth-century oolite cross head, decorated with hook-beaked birds, crouching lions, a griffin and other strange animals. The sides are covered with an unusual square Greek key pattern. It was discovered embedded in the south wall of the sanctuary in the eighteenth century, and is described by Nikolaus

Leicester's Tower, Evesham
This memorial to Simon de Montfort, Earl of Leicester, who fell in the battle of Evesham, 1265, was erected in 1840. His remains were buried in the Abbey Park, Evesham, where a plaque reads: 'This stone, brought from his birthplace, the Castle of Montfort-l'Amaury in France, was erected to commemorate the seven-hundredth anniversary of his death. Unveiled by the Speaker of the House of Commons and dedicated by His Grace the Archbishop of Canterbury on the 18th day of July 1965.'

Cropthorne Mill and Fladbury Weir
A small cable ferry operates between the two river banks, and on the Cropthorne side, beyond the island on which the mill stands, is Fladbury Lock. A plaque beside the lock reads: 'Empowered by a charter granted to him by King Charles the first on the 9th of March 1635, Wm Sandys of Fladbury made this River Avon navigable . . .' After becoming 'derelict', the 'Navigation' was re-opened on 10 June 1962.

Pevsner as being 'the best piece of Anglo-Saxon art in the county'.

The Avon is joined by the Merry Brook near Jubilee Bridge and, swinging south to Cropthorne, it loops around Fladbury and flows past Lower Moor and Upper Moor to Wyre Piddle. Like most of the villages alongside this stretch of the river, Wyre Piddle lies entirely on one bank with open countryside on the other.

The church, overlooking the waterway, is built

on the site of a prehistoric burial ground. It dates from the twelfth century, but was greatly restored in 1888. At the junction of Church Street and the Worcester Road stand the remains of an old wayside cross.

The gardens of the houses on the south side of the main road reach down to the Avon and many have private moorings. There are no public moorings in the village, but the Anchor Inn provides moorings for its customers.

At the eastern end of Wyre Piddle boating traffic has to negotiate Smith's Island and the quaintly named Tiddle Widdle 'Island', which is, in reality, attached to the bank.

Wyre Mill, half a mile downstream from the village, was called by Showell 'the ugliest mill, of which Avon is ashamed'. It is now owned by the Lower Avon Navigation Trust and has been converted into a social club for the exclusive use of members, who can also moor near by. In addition to the Trust's Office there is a maintenance wharf, reserved for working craft only. Wyre Lock is situated between the far southern bank and Wyre Island and can only be reached on foot through private land, although in season many anglers line the river's banks.

As the Avon heads south, through wide, willow-flanked meadows, the hills recede and gradually the buildings of Pershore begin to close in on the river. At Pershore Lock, the Georgian town stands at the

Cottages in Church Street, Wyre Piddle
The village's name is taken from the Piddle brook, which rises in the hills south of Redditch and flows into the Avon just below Wyre Mill.

water's edge and above the roof-tops rises the great pinnacled tower of its ancient abbey.

According to Camden, the name of Pershore is derived from the Anglo-Saxon word for pears, for which, along with Pershore plums, the town is renowned. Walls, however, considers that the name is derived from 'persche ora', meaning 'osier bank'; and Garrett declares that 'it is from "pursh", ancient Saxon for "willow"'.

Pershore, wrote Showell, is 'one of the few towns or villages that the river actually visits; these are usually found a little to the left, over a hill, or across the meadow, or behind the trees – never near, and seldom in sight'. But, with 'the river actually lapping the walls of the town', Pershore holds out a welcome that cannot be ignored.

CHAPTER 9

PERSHORE

In the summer of 1972 the people of Pershore and the surrounding villages held a series of celebrations, lasting from May to October. The opening service was held on 13 May in Pershore Abbey and sung by the choir of Westminster Abbey. The Dean of Westminster, Dr Eric Abbott, preached the sermon, reminding the assembled congregation of the special relationship between Pershore and Westminster Abbey, a relationship that stretches back to the eleventh century and continues to the present day. The celebrations, known as the 'Pershore Millennium', were held in honour of the one-thousandth anniversary of King Edgar's gift of a charter to Pershore Abbey in 972.

The charter was part of a general policy of monastic reform which applied to the entire kingdom. By the beginning of the tenth century the number of monks leading a religious way of life had declined dramatically. Dunstan, one of the signatories of the charter, had been appointed Abbot of Glastonbury in about 940 and had set up a community of monks based on the order founded by St Benedict in 529. The Benedictine Order experienced a great revival in Europe in the middle of the tenth century. Oswald, an Anglo-Danish member of the Order, was responsible for bringing the Benedictine way of life to the west Midlands: he replaced the secular priests of Worcester with monks in or about 964; he established a community at Deerhurst, on the banks of the Severn, about six years later; he founded the abbeys of Pershore and Winchcombe in 972 and the abbey of Evesham in 975. The newly founded abbeys came under the direct patronage and protection of the king and queen.

Pershore Abbey
Despite its relatively small size, medieval Pershore was a divided town. There were four separate manorial courts: two belonging to Pershore Abbey and two to Westminster Abbey. The friction between these two great religious landowners affected the whole life of the town, yet they governed the affairs of the town extremely well. Monastic control of Pershore came to an end in 1540, when the abbey was demolished, except for the choir, tower and south transept of the church.

During the period of political confusion following King Edgar's death in 975 the Benedictine monks were ejected from Pershore Abbey, probably by Alderman Aelfhere of Mercia, who confiscated many of the Pershore estates and claimed them as his own. However, they were reinstated in 983 when Aelfhere suffered a horrible death, 'eaten up by vermin' (Laird).

Odda was Aelfhere's grandson and he dedicated the Saxon chapel at Deerhurst to the memory of his brother, Aelfric, who was buried at Pershore. Odda was also a benefactor of Pershore Abbey and is reputed to have bought, for £100, some of the bones of St Eadburga for the monastery.

Eadburga, daughter of Edward the Elder and granddaughter of Alfred the Great, was attracted to the religious way of life from childhood. She became a

The Old Bridge, Pershore
During the Middle Ages the bridge was in a continual state of bad repair. One bank belonged to the Abbot of Westminster, the other to the Abbot of Pershore. Neither party felt that it was their duty to maintain the bridge despite a ruling making its upkeep their joint responsibility. Today, the Dean and Chapter of Westminster pay the county council to keep the bridge in good repair.

nun, entered a convent at Winchester and died there in 960. When her bones were installed at Pershore Abbey several miracles took place and her shrine became a minor centre for pilgrimage.

The first abbot, Foldbriht, died in 988. Legend tells that after his death, as his body lay awaiting burial, he suddenly sat up. The monks who were keeping vigil fled in terror; all except Abbot Germanus of Winchcombe. He stood his ground and ordered the spirit, in the name of the Lord, to tell him whether it came from heaven or hell. The spirit answered by saying that in heaven he had been found to be a sinner by St Benedict but, because of the prayers of St Oswald, the founder of the original monastery, his sins had been forgiven. His mission was evidently to inform the world that Oswald was one of the greatest saints that had ever lived. After 'half a day', the spirit departed.

Odda became a monk before he died in 1056, and, like his brother Aelfric, he was buried at Pershore. He had intended that his lands, which had belonged to Pershore in King Edgar's reign, should be returned to the monastery on his death, but instead they reverted, as was usual, to the king, at that time Edward the Confessor.

Edward decided to build a great church beside his palace at Westminster and, in December 1065, only eight days before he died, Westminster Abbey was consecrated. In his zeal he confiscated much of the land at Pershore and gave it to Westminster. The monks retaliated by closing the abbey church to Westminster's tenants in Pershore and so, in order not to aggravate the situation further, the monks of Westminster built the church of St Andrew.

At the time of Edgar's charter Pershore Abbey owned land not only in the town but also over a vast area of the west Midlands. By the time that the Domesday Book was completed most of this land had been lost.

The earliest part of the abbey church at Pershore had been constructed by 1086 and would have overshadowed the timber houses and monastic buildings of the town. The manor-house was the administrative centre of the Westminster estates, while the monastery controlled those remaining to Pershore.

Pershore was situated at a strategic point by a bridge over the Avon on the London-to-Worcester road. During the Civil War the bridge commanded one of the main routes to Wales. It was pulled down in 1644 by the army of Charles I, as it fled to Worcester from Oxford pursued by the Parliamentarian army of Sir William Waller.

Tragically, during its hasty demolition, the bridge collapsed and forty men were killed. A week later, when the Parliamentarian army of Waller attempted to cross the bridge, there was a similar accident. 'The great stone bridge being pulled down by the inhabitants after they had demolished the arches the rest suddenly tumbled down, whereby about sixty of the workmen were knocked on the head or drowned.'

In medieval Pershore the monks controlled, among other things, the market, the mill, the quarries, the bakehouse and the brewery, and paid the wages of their workers. They administered fines and they settled disputes. They even regulated the behaviour of their tenants, who were forbidden to play unlawful games like tennis, football and dice, and were expected to keep the streets and the gutters clean.

On the eve of the Dissolution the monastery was heavily in debt and relations with the townsfolk and neighbouring villagers were not helped by the ruthlessness of the last abbot, John Stonywell.

In the abbey's closing years one of the monks, Richard Beerley, sent Thomas Cromwell, the principal architect of the Reformation in England, a letter describing the state of the abbey, saying that 'the religion which we do observe and keep is no rule of Saint Benedict, nor is it no commandment of God, nor of no saint, but lies and foul ceremonies'.

It is thought that Beerley may have been encouraged by Cromwell to provide evidence that could form the basis of the monastery's dissolution.

Monastic control of the town came to an end on 21 January 1540 when, following the dissolution of Evesham Abbey by a few days, the monastery at Pershore was surrendered to Henry VIII. Quite suddenly a chapter in the

history of the Vale of Evesham had drawn to a close. For Pershore, and for Evesham, it was the end of a way of life that had lasted for more than five hundred years.

The site of Pershore monastery with its manor, lands and fair was granted to Anthony Southwell and the nave to the parishioners. The townsfolk, however, exchanged the nave for the choir and transepts. The rest was demolished. Two massive buttresses were erected in 1686 to support the fourteenth-century tower after the collapse of the north transept. The pinnacles were added to the tower in 1871 and the flying buttresses in 1913. All that now remains of the abbey and its extensive monastic buildings are the choir, tower and south transept of the church and the almonry, near by.

PERSHORE TO TEWKESBURY

The prosperity of Pershore was considerably enhanced after William Sandys of Fladbury had made the Avon navigable in the mid seventeenth century.

In 1759 the Lower Avon Navigation was purchased by George Perrott, a wealthy London lawyer who became a judge in the Court of Exchequer four years later. He was responsible for building Perrott House in Bridge Street, 'the finest house in Pershore', and retired there in 1775 because of ill health. The navigation rights were inherited by his nephew, George, who built Craycombe House, near Fladbury.

During the mid nineteenth century, the arrival of the railways resulted in the decline of transport by river and canal. By 1870 only three barges a month were calling at Pershore.

The Perrott family or their trustees retained the navigation rights of the Lower Avon until 1924, when they were bought by the Lower Avon Navigation Company Limited. After the Second World War, before restoration by the Lower Avon Navigation Trust, the river was unnavigable above Pershore.

Half a mile east of Pershore Lock is Wick and, standing to the north-west of the rebuilt church, Wick Manor. The village contains some fine examples of black and white timber-framed cottages.

Below the ancient, six-arched Pershore Bridge, now bypassed by a reinforced concrete bridge built in 1928, the Avon 'writhes like a wounded snake' (Thorne) to Strensham.

On this part of the river lies Pensham, a long, straggling, isolated village, surrounded by open fields and containing a few black and white cottages. Pensham Fields Farm belongs to Pershore College of Horticulture.

To the west of the village and on the opposite bank is Tiddesley Wood, which until the Dissolution was the Abbot of Westminster's deer park. It was here, in 1833, that the landlord of the Butcher's Arms in Pershore discovered a wild plum from which the Pershore or Egg Plum was developed.

As the Avon leaves Pershore and the Vale of Evesham, the countryside adjoining the river begins to revert, once again, to mixed farming. Ten miles or so to the west is the dark silhouette of the Malvern Hills. On the opposite horizon is the tree-swathed escarpment of the Cotswolds. Between them, rises Bredon Hill.

Eckington Bridge, considered to be the oldest bridge on the Avon
Quiller-Couch observed that the red sandstone bridge of six irregular arches seemed 'as old as Avon itself' and noticed that 'many deep grooves or notches ran across it. They were marks worn in the stone by the tow-ropes of departed barges'. He later wrote a poem entitled 'Upon Eckington Bridge, Rive Avon'.

The twin villages of Great and Little Comberton lie on its northern slopes. Both anciently belonged to the Abbey of Westminster. After the Dissolution they were held by the Beauchamps of Warwick, who also owned Elmley Castle.

Great Comberton stands on rising ground two and a half miles south of Pershore. Quay Lane leads from the riverside moorings up through orchards and farmland to the village. *Cumbrincgtune*, as it was known in the tenth century, derives its name from *Cumbra*, an Anglo-Saxon personal name, and means 'the town of Cumbra's family or descendants'.

Both villages have now been swelled by new housing development. But the thatched cottages still retain their old-world charm, their black and white, timber-framed walls bedecked in summertime with honeysuckle, clematis and rambling roses.

Little Comberton lies to the north-east of Great Comberton, the towers of their stone churches keeping a neighbourly eye on each other across the fields. The manor of Little Comberton and the seventeenth-century timber-framed Nash's Farm-house, north of the church, are both fine buildings.

One mile south-east of Little Comberton is Bricklehampton, famed for having the longest place name in Britain with fourteen letters of the alphabet, none of them repeated.

Elmley Castle, nestling on the northern wooded slopes of Bredon Hill, is half a mile away. Although the Revd Lloyd stated in 1967 that 'the principal occupation of the village is market gardening', very few of the villagers today are employed on the land.

In addition to Elmley Castle's three public houses, there is a cider mill, a pottery, a builder's firm and a joinery. The post office and shop closed in 1984.

The oldest parts of the church of St Mary are the nave and chancel, dating from the eleventh and twelfth centuries. The church contains a beautifully carved seventeenth-century alabaster memorial to the Savage family. There is also a large memorial to the first Earl of Coventry, erected by his second wife, who later married Thomas Savage. The Savage family purchased the manor of Elmley Castle from Henry VIII in 1544 and shortly after built their mansion behind the church. It was held by them until the early part of the nineteenth century.

The castle at Elmley stood on a mound high on the slopes of Bredon Hill. It was built shortly after the Norman Conquest.

The Revd Lloyd thinks that its strategic position, overlooking the Avon valley between Pershore and Evesham, may have been instrumental in the defeat of Simon de Montfort at the battle of Evesham. The castle belonged to the Beauchamps, loyal supporters of Henry III, and from the moment the baron's army under de Montfort crossed the Malverns it would have been under constant observation.

The Beauchamps were rewarded by the king, and he inhabitants of Elmley Castle were granted the privilege of holding certain markets and fairs. The stone cross at the entrance to the village is thought o have been the market centre and the main road, eading to the church, is exceptionally wide because t had to accommodate the buyers, the sellers and he livestock.

William, a son of 'Lord Beauchamp', inherited he estate at Warwick from his uncle William Maudit in 1268 and became the ninth Earl of Warwick. The chief seat of the Beauchamps was hen transferred to Warwick Castle and the castle at Elmley fell into ruins. The stone was used by the villagers in the building of their houses and church and some of it was taken to Pershore for the construction of the six-arched bridge.

South of the ancient bridge is Birlingham. Robert Eyres Landor, the younger brother of Walter Savage Landor, was parson here for forty years until his death in 1869. He wrote *The Count Arezzi*, a tragedy published anonymously in 1824, which was believed by the public to have been written by Byron. Its success was brief, however, for when Landor announced his authorship, demand immediately ceased.

From the church of St James and the tiny village green close by, a road (later becoming a long and pot-holed dirt track) leads down to the Avon and Nafford Lock.

Downstream from Great Comberton, Nafford with its few houses, lock and weir is said to be the prettiest spot on the Lower Avon.

Thomas Habington, the Worcestershire historian (1560–1647), mentions the ancient village of Nafford which was included in the Domesday survey of 1086: 'On the aspiring height of Bredon Hill stood Nafford church, where St Catherine was in former ages honoured.' He then says that 'Nafford lyeth now interred without a monument', and it is thought that the village may have been buried by a landslide. No trace of it remains. However, evidence of the small chapel and well of St Catherine can be found immediately below the tower on Bredon Hill.

Midway between the tower and Nafford Lock is

The abbey and weir, Pershore

Before his death in 1780 Perrott described trade on the Avon: 'Divers large quantities of coals were brought up the said river Avon and landed at Evesham and Stratford . . . and great quantities of corn and grain were brought from the county of Oxford to Evesham and Stratford and there and at other mills upon the said river ground into flour and sent down the said river to Bristol and other places up and down the Severn . . .'

Aerial view of Bredon Hill with Tiddesley Wood, Pensham and Great Comberton

In his early-twentieth-century guidebook, Round Bredon Hill, Packer wrote that Great Comberton, 'like its sister village, Little Comberton, is situated in the midst of the extensive orchards of the Evesham vale, which in May's festive month are gay with delicate pink and white blossoms, and, later on, at the plum and apple harvest, are no less colourful'.

Woollas Hall, a high, gabled stone mansion built in 1611 and surrounded by stately trees.

Although it is now divided into apartments, Woollas Hall still retains its Jacobean staircase and minstrels' gallery.

In his *Rural Rides*, William Cobbett described the view of the Avon and Severn valleys from Bredon Hill as 'one of the very richest spots of England, and I am fully convinced, a richer spot than is to be seen in any other country in the world'.

Below Nafford Lock the Avon forms a series of acute bends, the final one of which is known as the Swan's Neck. From Birlingham Wharf, a footpath leads across the meadows of the northern bank to Birlingham village. Half a mile downstream, below Eckington Wharf, is Eckington Bridge.

The village of Eckington is about half a mile from the bridge. Archaeological excavation has revealed evidence of a Roman settlement to the north-west. The place name is Saxon and means 'the town of Eck's family'.

On the main street of Eckington there is a stone cross reputed to be older than the Norman church. (The top was added in the reign of Queen Victoria.) It was used as a preaching cross by the monks of Pershore Abbey.

The church of the Holy Trinity, the earliest parts dating from the twelfth century, contains several monuments to the Hanford family of nearby Woollas Hall.

A short distance downstream from Eckington Bridge the Avon is joined by the Bow Brook. The low-lying land here is liable to flooding and the willow-hung water-meadows, grazed by sheep, are particularly lush.

Defford, its name derived from 'deep ford', contains a large number of modern houses with a few black and white, timber-framed cottages, mainly situated near the church.

One mile north of Defford, in the village of

The Main Street, Elmley Castle

Elmley is derived from the word 'elm' and the Anglo-Saxon word leah and means 'the elm by the rough pasture land'. The great elms were killed by Dutch elm disease in the 1970s. The village has been labelled one of the ten prettiest villages in England and has about five hundred inhabitants.

Besford, is the only timber-framed church in the old county of Worcestershire. The chancel – a nineteenth-century addition – is built of stone, but the small church retains its sixteenth-century rood-loft. (Most of them were destroyed during the iconoclastic years of Edward VI.)

The Avon, now some fifty feet wide, sweeps in a mile-long curve around the village of Eckington and arrives at Strensham Lock. The Victorian red-brick lock-keeper's cottage, situated on an island beside the lock, was bought by the Lower Avon Navigation Trust in 1952. At the time of purchase it was derelict, but has now been made habitable.

Perched high on the wooded ridge above the lock is Strensham church, dedicated to St John the Baptist. It contains some fine monuments to the

Russells, who owned the manor at Strensham for about four hundred years. Their last lineal descendant died in 1774 and, like the family, their great moated house has gone.

In contrast to the rich and ornate monuments of the Russells there is a simple wall tablet in memory of Samuel Butler, the author of *Hudibras*, whose father was one of their tenants.

Butler was born in the year 1612 to Samuel and Mary Butler and baptized in the church on 14 February. His father was a farmer and a church-warden and was also employed by Sir John Russell, it is presumed as a clerk.

The family lived in a cottage, later known as 'Butler's Cot', and described by Thorne in about 1845 as 'a long low structure, very similar in kind to Anne Hathaway's cottage at Shottery.' It was still standing twenty-five years later but after falling into disrepair it was demolished.

Young Butler was educated at King's School, Worcester. He is thought to have become a clerk to 'one Mr Jefferys', probably Thomas Jefferey, 'of Earl's Croome, an Eminent Justice of the Peace for that County with whom he lived some years in an easy and no contemptible Service'. While at Earl's Croome it is said that he took up painting. Two of his portraits are still in existence, preserved in the church; the rest are reputed to have been used to stop up broken windows!

Butler spent most of his life in obscurity, as a clerk or secretary to a number of noble families. The experience gave him a valuable insight into religious bigotry and Puritan extremism during the years of the Commonwealth. It is thought that he began writing the first part of his satirical poem *Hudibras* in about 1653, when Oliver Cromwell was made Protector.

Butler, however, did not dare print the poem until after Cromwell's death. He was fifty when it was first published in 1663 and with it he achieved rapid, if temporary, success. Butler himself wrote of Charles II that:

> *He never ate, nor drank, nor slept,*
> *But* Hudibras *still near him kept;*
> *Nor would he go to church or so,*
> *But* Hudibras *must with him go.*

Yet, despite the king's liking for the work, Butler received nothing from him until fifteen years later, when he was granted a pension. By then, legend has it, Butler was living in poverty and neglect. At about this time, James Yonge wrote in his *Journal*: 'I saw the famous Mr Butler . . . an old paralytic claret drinker, a morose surly man, except elevated with claret, when he becomes very brisk and incomparable company.'

Butler died in 1680, at the age of sixty-seven, and was buried in the churchyard of St Paul's, Covent Garden.

East of Strensham is Bredon's Norton, a small village centred on the church of St Giles. The sixteenth-century manor-house, its gated archway dated 1585, was once the home of Sir Thomas Copley. He sailed to the New World with Sir Walter Raleigh and helped to found the state of Virginia.

More recently, the gabled house was owned by Mrs Victoria Woodhull Martin, who died in 1927 at the age of eighty-eight. An active campaigner for women's equal rights, she was the first woman to be nominated for the Presidency of the United States of America.

Norton Park, a large house dated 1830 and surrounded by 'a forest of noble trees', stands above the village on the luxuriant slopes of Bredon Hill.

BREDON HILL

The name Bredon is derived from the Celtic word *bre*, meaning a hill, and *dun*, meaning a down or open high ground. Bredon Hill is an isolated outlier of the great oolite limestone mass of the Cotswolds. It dominates the Vale of Evesham for many miles and was a site of strategic importance.

The remains of an Iron Age hill-fort can be traced here and excavations have revealed the mutilated skeletons of fifty men.

The King and Queen Stones standing on the hill

The church of St James, Birlingham
The church was rebuilt in the nineteenth century with an unusual stair turret at one corner. The Norman chancel arch of the ancient church was re-erected and forms a unique gateway to the churchyard.

above Westmancote were once the site for the meeting of the local manorial court. In the early nineteenth century it was recorded that one old inhabitant of Eckington remembered that, prior to the holding of the court, it was the custom to whitewash the stones. One theory is that this may have been the unconscious survival of an ancient fertility rite.

On the summit of the hill, standing beside the Banbury Stone, is a square stone edifice known as the Tower or Parson's Folly, built in the eighteenth century as a summer-house and look-out. It is said that Mr Parsons of Kemerton Court had it made thirty-nine feet high because he was determined to raise the height of Bredon Hill from 961 feet above sea-level to exactly 1,000 feet.

What gives the villages of Bredon Hill their character, and sets them apart from the low-lying villages of the Vale, is the honey-gold limestone of the buildings. Although isolated, villages like Overbury belong not to the surrounding plain but to the Cotswolds.

On a clear day, it is possible to see from the top to the Mendip Hills in the south, the Black Mountains to the west, and the Vale of Worcester to the north.

The church of St John the Baptist, Strensham
Within the church, the magnificent brasses and monuments to the Russell family, who owned the manor at Strensham for some four hundred years, are of particular interest because they depict the changes in costume of both men and women from 1375 onwards.

Bredon, which takes its name from the hill, stands on the east bank of the Avon and at Mill End there are moorings, a boatyard and a caravan site.

The village itself is ancient. In the eighth century, Eanwulf, grandfather of King Offa of Mercia, founded a monastery here, which came to own a great deal of land to the north. The estate gradually declined until the monastery was reduced to little more than a rich parish church. By 1086 the manor of Bredon, with its grange and park, was in the possession of the bishops of Worcester, to whom it belonged until the Dissolution.

The great barn at Bredon was built of oak and Cotswold stone for the bishops in the mid fourteenth century. It was given to the National Trust by Mr G.S. Cottrell in 1951, and was extensively restored after a disastrous fire which occurred on the night of 18 April 1980.

The church of St Giles, dating from the twelfth century, stands near the site of the ancient Saxon monastery founded by Eanwulf, which was destroyed by the Danes in about 850. The tower and slender spire, 161 feet high, is a landmark for many miles around.

A number of fine buildings are situated round the church, including the Elizabethan stone rectory, the seventeenth-century brick Old Mansion House and the eighteenth-century stone Manor House. In the centre of the village are the Reed Almshouses, a one-storey block of seventeenth-century stone houses forming three sides of a quadrangle.

After leaving Bredon, the Avon glides on to Twyning Fleet, with its moorings, small green, large caravan site and pleasant riverside inn.

The lane beside the Fleet Inn leads to Twyning Green. The houses around the green are mainly modern. But there are a few black and white timber-framed cottages near the red-brick school; Bird's Farm, close by, is particularly attractive.

Twyning, to the west of Twyning Green, has attracted more than its fair share of modern housing development. The older properties are near the Norman church of St Mary Magdalene, which was restored in 1868. Within the vicinity of the Twynings there are a surprising number of large manor-houses and farms.

A quarter of a mile downstream from Twyning Fleet, in a field at the edge of the river, is a spring called Chad Well, once renowned for its curative properties.

From here, for the final two miles of its journey to Tewkesbury, the Avon straightens almost into a line. It flows between broad, flat meadows and past extensive sand and gravel workings.

The high ground above the western bank is known as Mythe Hill. Mythe is an Old English word meaning 'river confluence'. It also gives its name to Mythe Bridge, a cast-iron structure of a single 170-foot span built by Thomas Telford in 1826, which crosses the Severn half a mile north-west of Tewkesbury. Near by, the Mythe Tute, or Royal Hill, is man-made, probably a look-out post built by the Saxons. All that remains of Mythe Manor House, now known as King John's Castle, is an ivy-covered tower. It is thought that the original building, demolished in 1539, is more likely to have been associated with Tewkesbury Abbey than with King John, who would have occupied Holme Castle: a fortress which once stood near where the River Swilgate joins the Avon.

Below Tewkesbury Marina, with its boatyard and slipways, the Avon is joined by Carrant Brook and then arrives at King John's Bridge, rebuilt in concrete and stone in 1962.

Not far from here

Avon's friendly streams with Severn join,
And Tewkesbury's walls, renowned for trophies,
shine.

Camden, translated by John Leland

Banbury Stone on the summit of Bredon Hill
It has been suggested that this large slab of oolite rock (now split into smaller lumps) was once used for human sacrifices. One of the larger pieces is known as the Elephant Stone, because it resembles a kneeling elephant. There is a tradition that on certain nights, when the bells of Pershore Abbey strike midnight, the stone moves down the hillside to drink from the Avon.

CHAPTER 10
TEWKESBURY

Tewkesbury, according to S. Rudder's *A New History of Gloucestershire*, published in 1779, is situated 'in a rich vale . . . watered by four rivers, like the garden of Eden'.

These four rivers are the Severn, the Avon, and two small streams, the Swilgate and the Carrant Brook, which flow into the Avon, one at either end of the town.

Tewkesbury takes its name from Theoc, a local seventh-century hermit. In 715 two Mercian dukes, Odda and Dodda, founded a small Benedictine monastery on the same site. In the ninth century, the monastery was ravaged by Danish invaders and twice destroyed by fire.

After the Norman Conquest, the manor of Tewkesbury was granted to Robert FitzHamon, a cousin of William Rufus. FitzHamon, together with Giraldus, Abbot of Cranbourne, founded a monastery in 1092 and, in 1121, it was consecrated as an abbey. Before it was dissolved in 1540, Tewkesbury Abbey had become one of the wealthiest religious houses in England. Its possessions, listed on seventy-four skins of parchment, were seized by the Crown. The church was condemned as superfluous but the town's inhabitants persuaded Henry VIII to sell them the abbey church and churchyard for £453, the estimated value of the lead on the roof and the metal from the bells.

The fertile soil around Tewkesbury contributed greatly to the wealth of the abbey. The Domesday Book recorded two mills; by the late sixteenth century the number had increased to four.

View of Tewkesbury, the abbey and the Mill Avon from the air

'The water is out at Tewkesbury' is a local saying which refers to the fact that after heavy and continuous rain the rivers are liable to flood the surrounding meadows. Particularly vulnerable is the Ham, the wide expanse of flat green land lying between the Severn and the Mill Avon.

There has been a mill on the site of Healing's Mill since the thirteenth century. The current mill was built in 1865 by Samuel Healing and was steam-powered. It switched to electricity in the 1950s and in 1976 it was rebuilt and modernized, retaining its nineteenth-century brick exterior. It has been owned by Allied Mills since 1961 and is one of the largest inland flour mills in England. The mill receives some of its grain by barge from the Bristol Channel ports.

Abbey Mill stands on the Mill Avon waterfront, and is now used to stage medieval banquets.

The Tudor House Hotel was the home of John Moore, born in Tewkesbury in 1907, whose amusing novels are about the local countryside. The John Moore Museum (opened in 1980) is housed in a restored row of medieval half-timbered cottages, which stand in front of the abbey in Church Street. The museum works closely with the Gloucestershire Trust for Nature Conservation.

The eighteenth-century Hop Pole Inn is also in Church Street; after a visit by Queen Mary in the 1920s, the word 'Royal' was added to the name. It was mentioned by Charles Dickens in *The Pickwick Papers* and, consequently, has a Pickwick Bar and Dickens Room.

The town's growth was restricted by the flooding of its four rivers and the Tudor builders worked upwards rather than outwards, constructing three- and four-storey houses fronting the main streets. Crammed behind these large houses were rows of cottages, in a warren of alleys and courts. Today only the passageways remain.

Although Tewkesbury contains a wealth of interesting buildings, it is more famous for the battle which took place in Bloody Meadow, south of the abbey, on 4 May 1471.

The rival armies, Yorkist and Lancastrian, met where the Avon joins the Severn. There is a tradition that Queen Margaret, wife of Henry VI, watched the battle from the top of the abbey tower. The queen had handed over command to Edmund Beaufort, Duke of Somerset, who also controlled the

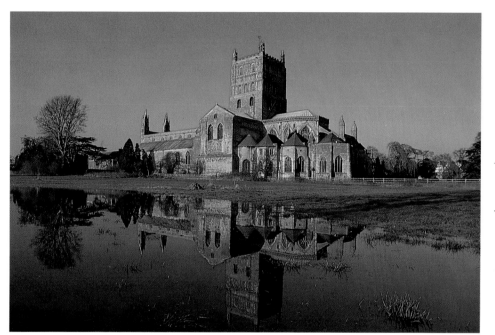

Tewkesbury Abbey and the River Swilgate in flood
Built by the Benedictine monks at the beginning of the twelfth century, the abbey stood on elevated ground within the triangle formed by the rivers Severn, Old Avon and Swilgate. Swilgate is derived from the Old English word swillan, *meaning 'to wash or rinse'. The gate was probably a floodgate. The magnificent abbey church was saved from demolition by the town's inhabitants. The tower is forty-six feet square and 148 feet high to the top of the pinnacles.*

right wing. Her son Edward, Prince of Wales, was in command of the centre supported by John Lord Wenlock who, unfortunately, had a reputation for changing sides. Against them, Edward IV, son of Richard of York, was supported on the left flank by his brother, Richard of Gloucester, and on the right by the Marquis of Dorset and Lord Hastings.

Somerset led his men into the wooded cover of Tewkesbury Park and attempted to surprise Edward's forces. He had left orders with Wenlock to attack as soon as his soldiers emerged from the trees. But Edward had anticipated the plan and had dispatched 200 spearmen to the spot. Gloucester also saw the danger and advanced against Somerset. Wenlock failed to come to Somerset's aid; the duke's men were forced to retreat and many were killed.

According to Holinshed, Richard tried a ruse. He turned his army and fled. The Lancastrians followed. Edward's division entered the abandoned camp and routed the remaining defenders. Richard, seeing that Somerset's escape was barred, turned his men once more into the offensive. The Lancastrians who escaped slaughter fled to the abbey and were given refuge.

Edward's men were refused entry until a promise was made to spare the soldiers' lives. Once this was given, the defeated men emerged from the abbey only to be butchered in the grounds. Many Lancastrians were killed or drowned as they tried to escape across the Avon and most of their leaders were killed. Somerset and the few surviving nobles were captured and, after a summary trial, executed in the market-place.

Bloody Meadow is so called after the dreadful massacre there on that fateful day in May. The Avon was so full of corpses that the water became, in Shakespeare's words, 'Alas, a crimson river of warm blood'.

So the river which rises in the blood of the battle of Naseby ends in the blood of the battle of Tewkesbury. But the Avon's journey is not quite over.

From the northern outskirts of Tewkesbury the river divides: the Old Avon rushes over a weir to join the Severn more than a mile earlier than the Mill Avon. Both pass under King John's Bridge (or its extension Beaufort Bridge) and run parallel to each other until they meet briefly at Avon Lock, the gateway to the Severn and the sea.

The Mill Avon runs along the western edge of the town, past Tolsey Wharf and a row of attractive black and white, timber-framed houses overlooking the water, to the Abbey Mill. The River Swilgate flows south through the abbey grounds and enters the Mill Avon at the southern end of the town.

Bloody Meadow lies immediately south of the tiny stream, near its confluence with the Mill Avon. A sewage works, screened by trees, now occupies part of the battle site.

The Avon, however, culminates not in the noise and tumult of battle. If it dies, it dies silently and, without a murmur, it is reborn as the Severn.

Avon waterfront
The Avon divides near King John's Bridge: the Old Avon flows over a weir, under Beaufort Bridge and past Healing's Mill, to take the shorter route to the Severn; the Mill Avon, probably cut by the monks in the twelfth century to power Abbey Mill, flows under King John's Bridge and along the western edge of the town, to enter the Severn near Bloody Meadow.

Photographic Notes

Shakespeare's Avon officially rises in the upland village of Naseby and it was near there on a bleak January evening that my work on this project began.

The first signs of the Avon appeared in a field, most of which was covered in snow. The water, partially frozen, appeared quite still and only on close examination could its trickling form be detected. The solitude seemed quite intense, and yet it is also very fitting that such a historic river should have such a quiet and peaceful start.

Research for photographs is all important and to have experienced this lonely setting prepared me very nicely for a project I knew would be something special.

Most of the locations were visited many times throughout the year in order that the best could be obtained from each area, and the final result could have the variety of mood and colour so necessary to represent the Avon's changing journey.

Landscapes can be photographed at various times of the day according to personal preference, but where possible I generally chose to work in the low light of morning or evening, which offered better modelling and warmer colours.

The towns unfortunately offered no such flexibility and had to be photographed when the light was most suitably on the buildings, and very often this was when they were at their busiest.

The equipment used was a 35mm Nikon: an F3 body plus motor-drive and a variety of lenses from 24mm to 600mm. Filters were used only occasionally, but consisted of a polarizer, to control reflections and saturate colours; an 81B to warm the coolish light sometimes found at midday and a graduated grey filter to darken skies. A medium-sized Gitzo tripod was used where necessary for slow shutter speeds, long lenses and as an aid to considered composition.

I used Fuji 50 and 100 film and occasionally Kodachrome 25.

The aerial photographs were taken from a Jet Ranger helicopter with the door removed, and when the sun was low in the sky. Lenses were 35mm and 85mm and the shutter speeds were a 500th of a second plus to avoid camera shake.

Many photographers, amateur or professional, offer their best when working on a series of pictures with a linking theme. For my best shots I often find myself inexplicably drawn to water: its ever-changing form offering immeasurable possibilities.

The change in Shakespeare's Avon was most apparent from the air, where its course could be traced and followed easily and quickly. As it neared the lovely town of Tewkesbury the Avon was wide and powerful, dominating the landscape below as though it had grown with the history it had collected, and was proudly showing it before joining forces with the Severn to head for the open sea.

The year I have spent photographing the Avon's journey from source to Severn has been extremely enjoyable. I would recommend it to anyone.

Rob Talbot

Properties Open to the Public

NASEBY

Naseby Battle and Farm
    Museum
Purlieu Farm
Naseby
Northamptonshire
Telephone: (0604) 740241
Open: Easter to end of
September

NASEBY TO RUGBY

Stanford Hall
Lutterworth
Leicestershire
LE17 6DH
Telephone: (0788) 860250
Open: Easter to end of
September, Thursdays,
Saturdays, Sundays and also
Bank Holiday Mondays and
Tuesdays

RUGBY TO COVENTRY

Coombe Abbey Country Park
Brinklow Road
Binley
nr Coventry
CV3 2AB
Telephone: Ranger's Office
(0203) 453720

COVENTRY

Coventry Cathedral and
    Visitors' Centre
7 Priory Row
Coventry
CV1 5ES
Telephone: (0203) 24323/27597
Open throughout the year

COVENTRY TO KENILWORTH

Stoneleigh Abbey
Kenilworth
Warwickshire
Telephone: (0926) 52116
No information at the time of
going to press – the estate was
put on the market in 1988

KENILWORTH

Kenilworth Castle
Kenilworth
Warwickshire
Open throughout the year
except Christmas Eve,
Christmas Day, Boxing Day
and New Year's Day

WARWICK

Warwick Castle
Warwick
CV34 4QU
Telephone: (0926) 495421
Open every day except
Christmas Day

Lord Leycester Hospital
Warwick
CV34 4BH
Telephone: (0926)
491422/492797
Open throughout the year
except Sundays, Good Friday
and Christmas Day

WARWICK TO STRATFORD-UPON-AVON

Charlecote Park
Wellesbourne
Warwick
CV35 9ER
Telephone: (0789) 840277
Open: May to end September
except Mondays and Thursdays;
April and October open
Saturdays and Sundays

STRATFORD-UPON-AVON

Birthplace
Henley Street
Stratford-upon-Avon
Warwickshire
Telephone: (0789) 204016
Open throughout the year
except Christmas Eve,
Christmas Day and Boxing Day

Anne Hathaway's Cottage
Shottery
Stratford-upon-Avon
Warwickshire
Telephone: (0789) 292100
Open throughout the year
except Christmas Eve,
Christmas Day and Boxing Day

Hall's Croft
Old Town
Stratford-upon-Avon
Warwickshire
Telephone: (0789) 292107
Open throughout the year
except Sundays from
November to March and
Christmas Eve, Christmas Day
and Boxing Day

Mary Arden's House and
    Countryside Museum
Wilmcote
Stratford-upon-Avon
Telephone: (0789) 293455
Open throughout the year,
except Sundays from
November to March

New Place and Nash's House
Chapel Street
Stratford-upon-Avon
Telephone: (0789) 292325
Open throughout the year,
except Sundays from
November to March and
Christmas Eve, Christmas Day
and Boxing Day

King Edward VI Grammar
    School
Church Street
Stratford-upon-Avon
CV37 6HB
Telephone: (0789) 293351
Open occasionally during
school holidays

Holy Trinity Church
Old Town
Stratford-upon-Avon
Telephone: The Parish Office
(0789) 66316
Open throughout the year

Tourist Information Offices and Other Useful Addresses

RUGBY

Tourist Information Office
The Library
St Matthews Street
Rugby
Warwickshire
CV21 3BZ
Telephone: (0788) 535348

COVENTRY

Tourist Information Office
Central Library
Smithford Way
Coventry
CV1 1FY
Telephone: (0203) 832312

KENILWORTH

Tourist Information Office
The Library
Smalley Place
Kenilworth
Warwickshire
CV8 1QG
Telephone: (0926) 52595

ROYAL LEAMINGTON SPA

Tourist Information Office
Jephson Lodge
The Parade
Royal Leamington Spa
Warwickshire
CV32 4UR
Telephone: (0926) 311470

WARWICK

Tourist Information Office
The Court House
Jury Street
Warwick
Telephone: (0926) 492212

STRATFORD-UPON-AVON

Tourist Information Office
1 High Street
Stratford-upon-Avon
Warwickshire
CV37 6AU
Telephone: (0789) 293127
The Shakespeare Birthplace
   Trust
The Shakespeare Centre
Stratford-upon-Avon
Warwickshire
CV37 6QW
Telephone: (0789) 204016

Royal Shakespeare Theatre,
   Swan Theatre and The
   Other Place
For all bookings telephone:
(0789) 295623
24-hour booking information:
(0789) 69191
Season: end March to end
January

EVESHAM

(summer only)
Tourist Information Office
The Almonry Museum
Abbey Gate
Evesham
Worcestershire
WR11 4BG
Telephone: (0386) 6944

PERSHORE

Tourist Information Office
Council Offices
37 High Street
Pershore
Worcester
WR10 1AH
Telephone: (0386) 554711

TEWKESBURY

(summer only)
Tourist Information Office
64 Barton Street
Tewkesbury
Gloucestershire
GL20 5PX
Telephone: (0684) 295027

THE NATIONAL TRUST

Regional Information Office
The National Trust
Severn Regional Office
Mythe End House
Tewkesbury
Gloucestershire
GL20 6EB
Telephone: (0684) 850051

WARWICKSHIRE NATURE CONSERVATION TRUST

Montague Road
Warwick
CV34 5LW
Telephone: (0926) 496848

Select Bibliography

Barrett, Philip, and Wilson, Marshall, *The Book of Pershore*, Buckingham, Barracuda, 1980

Baxter, Eric G., *Dr Jephson of Leamington Spa*, Warwickshire Local History Society, 1980

Bird, John, *Stratford-upon-Avon Official Guide*, Stratford District Council, 1976

Booth, D.T.N., *Warwickshire Watermills*, Midland Wind and Waterways Group, 1978

Burbidge, F. Bliss, *Old Coventry and Lady Godiva*, Birmingham, Cornish Brothers, 1952

Butler, Samuel, *Hudibras*, ed. John Wilders, Clarendon Press, 1967 (first published 1663, 1664, 1678)

Cash, J. Allan, *Shakespeare's Avon*, Chapman & Hall, 1949

Davies, J. Rees, *Rugby as it was*, Hendon, 1979

Drew, John H., *Kenilworth: A Manor of the King*, Kenilworth, Pleasaunce, 1971

Drew, John H., *The Book of Royal Leamington Spa*, Buckingham, Barracuda, 1978

Drewry, J., *The History of Guy, Earl of Warwick*, 1796

Dugdale, Sir William, *The Antiquities of Warwickshire*, (revised and augmented by Dr W. Thomas), London, 1730

Fairfax-Lucy, Alice, Lady, *Charlecote and the Lucys*, Jarrold, 1982

Field, William, *An Historical and Descriptive Account of the Town and Castle of Warwick and the Neighbouring Spa of Leamington*, Sharpe, 1815

Fox, Levi, *Coventry's Heritage*, Coventry Evening Telegraph, 1957

Fox, Levi, *Historic Stratford-upon-Avon*, Norwich, Jarrold, 1986

Fox, Levi, *The Shakespearian Properties*, Norwich, Jarrold, 1981

Garrett, John Henry, *The Idyllic Avon*, Putnam, 1906

Gates, P.J.E., *Warwick in Times Past*, Countryside, 1986

Gateway to the Avon, The Lower Avon Navigation Trust, 1984

Gibbons, W.G., *The Royal Baths and Pump Rooms: Royal Leamington Spa*, 1980

Greenall, R.L., *Naseby: A Parish History*, Leicester, University of Leicester, 1974

Holinshed, Raphael, *Chronicles*, 1586

Hutchings, David, and Higgins, David, *The Upper Avon Navigation Guide*, Hutchings, n.d.

Ireland, Samuel, *Picturesque Views on the Upper, or Warwickshire Avon*, Faulder, 1795

Jennett, Sean, ed., *The Shakespeare Country and South Warwickshire*, Darton, Longman & Todd, 1965

Kemp, Thomas, *A History of Warwick and its People*, Cooke, 1905

Kemp, Thomas, ed., *The Black Book of Warwick*, Cooke, 1895

Laird, F.C., *A Topographical and Historical Description of the County of Worcester*, London, 1814

Lines, Charles, *The Book of Warwick*, Buckingham, Barracuda, 1985

Lloyd, Revd R.H., *Bredon Hill and its Villages* (local guide), 1967

McKnight, Hugh, *The Shell Book of Inland Waterways*, Newton Abbot, David & Charles, 1975

Mastin, Revd John, *The History and Antiquities of Naseby in the County of Northamptonshire*, Cambridge, 1792

Mee, Arthur, *The King's England: Warwickshire*, Hodder & Stoughton, 1936

Moncrieff, W.T., *Excursion to Kenilworth*, Elliston, 1824

Moncrieff, W.T., *The Visitor's New Guide to the Spa of Leamington Priors*, Elliston, 1824

Moore, Robin, *A History of Coombe Abbey*, Coventry, Jones-Sands, 1983

Nash, J., *History and Antiquities of Worcestershire*, London, 1781–2

Packer, T.H., *Round Bredon Hill*, Cheltenham & London, Burrow, n.d.

Palmer, Roy, *The Folklore of Warwickshire*, Batsford, 1976

Pearson's Avon Ring Companion, Burton-on-Trent, Pearson, 1987

Pevsner, Nikolaus, revised by Bridget Cherry, *Northamptonshire* (Buildings of England series), Penguin Books, 1973

Pevsner, Nikolaus and Wedgwood, Alexandra, *Warwickshire* (Buildings of England series), Penguin Books, 1966

Pevsner, Nikolaus, *Worcestershire* (Buildings of England Series), Penguin Books, 1968

Poole, Benjamin, compiler, *Coventry: Its History and Antiquities*, Smith, 1870

Pringle, Roger, ed., *Poems of Warwickshire: An Anthology*, Kineton, Roundwood, 1980

Quiller-Couch, A.T., *The Warwickshire Avon*, Harper, 1891 (republished under the title *Exploring Shakespeare Country*, Ludlum, Stuart, D., ed., Thames & Hudson, 1985)

Renn, D.F., *Kenilworth Castle*, HMSO, 1973

Richardson, Kenneth, *Coventry: Past into Present*, Chichester, Phillimore, 1987

Ross, Kathleen, *The Book of Tewkesbury*, Buckingham, Barracuda, 1986

Rouse, W.H.D., *A History of Rugby School*, Duckworth, 1898

Shakespeare, William, *The Complete Works*, ed. Peter Alexander, Collins, 1951

Showell, Charles, *Shakespeare's Avon: From Source to Severn*, Simpkin, Marshall, Hamilton, Kent, 1901

Shurey, Richard, *Shakespeare's Avon from Source to Severn*, Whitethorn, 1981

Styles, Philip, *The Borough of Warwick*, Pitkin, 1973

Thorne, James, *Rambles by Rivers: The Avon*, Knight, 1845

Timmins, Sam, *A History of Warwickshire*, Stock, 1889

Verey, David, *Gloucestershire: The Vale and the Forest of Dean*, (Buildings of England series), Penguin Books, 1970

Victoria History of the County of Warwick, OUP

Victoria History of the County of Worcester, St Catherine Press, 1924

Walls, Ernest, *Shakespeare's Avon*, Arrowsmith, 1935

Warwick, Frances, Countess of, *Warwick Castle and its Earls*, Hutchinson, 1903

Index

Abbot's Salford 114, 116
Alveston 84, 90, 92, 94
Arrow (river) 113
Ashow 50, 51

Bagington 44
Barford 82, 85
Barton 110
Bengeworth 126
Besford 145
Bidford-on-Avon 109, 110, 113
Binton 109
Birlingham 143, 145, 147
Blackdown Mill 58
Blacklow Hill 58, 61, 76
Bosworth Mill Farm 17
Brandon 32, 33, 34, 35, 36
Bredon 148
Bredon Hill 117, 128, 129, 140, 142–4, 147–9
Bredon's Norton 147
Bretford 32
Bricklehampton 142
Brinklow 32, 35
Brownsover 21, 26, 28
Bubbenhall 44
Buckle Street 110

Catthorpe 20
Chad Well 149
Chadbury 128
Charlecote 85, 86, 87–90, 92, 93
Charlton 129, 131
Chesford Bridge 50, 58
Church Lawford 31, 32
Churchover 20, 23, 35

Cleeve Hill 114, 116
Cleeve Prior 113, 114
Clifford Chambers 106
Clifton-upon-Dunsmore 20, 21
Clopton House 94
Coombe Abbey 35, 36, 58
Copdock Hill 85
Cotswolds 106, 126, 140, 148
Coventry 21, 28, 32, 33, 36, 37, 39–43, 44, 46, 49, 65
Craycombe Hill 131
Cropthorne 131, 132

Dead Men's Ait 118
Defford 145
Dunsmore Heath 34, 36, 61

Eckington 140, 145, 147
Edge Hill 9, 90
Elmley Castle 142, 143, 145
Evesham 7, 54, 92, 109, 113, 114, 116–19, 121–5, 126, 128, 129, 131, 135, 138, 139, 142, 143

Fladbury 92, 131, 132, 140
Fosse Way 23, 32, 82
Fulbrook 82, 84

Gaveston's Cross 58, 61
Great Comberton 142–4
Guy's Cliffe 58–65

Hampton 128, 129
Hampton Lucy 86
Hampton Wood 84, 88
Harvington 116, 117

Hatton Rock 92
Hillborough 106, 109, 113
Hill Wootton 58

Kenilworth 20, 31, 44, 51, 53–7, 58, 60, 67, 78, 113, 124

King's Newnham 31, 32
King's Norton 105

Leam (river) 67, 68, 72
Leamington Priors 67, 68
Leamington Spa 51, 65, 67–70, 72
Leek Wootton 58
Lilbourne 20
Little Comberton 142, 144
Little Lawford 28, 30, 31, 35
Long Lawford 28, 31
Longbridge 82
Luddington 108
Lutterworth 21

Malvern Hills 140, 142
Marlcliff 110, 111, 113, 114
Marston 32
Mendip Hills 11, 148
Middle Littleton 116, 117
Motslow Hill 47
Mythe Hill 149

Nafford 143, 145
Naseby 7, 9–13, 14–16, 34, 154, 156
Newbold-on-Avon 28, 30, 31
Newnham Regis 31, 32
Newton 20, 35

North Kilworth 17, 18
North Littleton 117
Norton 117, 118

Offenham 118, 119, 126
Old Milverton 65, 72
Overbury 148

Pensham 140
Pershore 128, 133, 135–9, 140, 142, 143, 145, 149

Rugby 14, 20, 21, 23–7, 28, 32
Ryknild Street 110
Ryton-on-Dunsmore 36, 37, 44

Salford Hall 114
Salford Priors 113, 114
Scar Bank 85
Severn (river) 16, 21, 94, 143, 149, 151, 154, 156
Sherbourne 82, 84, 86
Shottery 99, 101, 146
South Kilworth 17
South Littleton 117
Sowe (river) 46, 47, 49
Stanford-on-Avon 18, 20
Stanford Hall 17–20
Stare Bridge 46
Stareton 46
Stoneleigh 7, 32, 44, 46, 47, 50
Stoneleigh Abbey 49, 50
Stour (river) 106
Stratford-upon-Avon 7, 9, 17, 26, 84, 90, 92–4, 97–105, 106, 108, 110, 111, 113, 114

Strensham 140, 145–8
Sulby Abbey 17
Swift (river) 21, 28
Swilgate (river) 151, 153, 154
Swinford 19

Tewkesbury 7, 89, 92, 94, 149, 151–4, 156
Thelsford Brook 85
Tiddesley Wood 140, 144
Tiddington 92
Twyning, Twyning Green, Twyning Fleet 148, 149

Vale of Evesham 34, 111, 119, 139, 140, 144, 147

Warwick 58, 61, 62, 65, 67, 70, 72, 75–81, 82, 90, 92, 143
Wasperton 84, 85, 89
Watling Street 20, 23
Welcombe Hills 93, 94
Welford 17
Welford-on-Avon 108, 109, 113, 119
Westmancote 147
Weston-on-Avon 108
Wick 140
Wickhamford 126
Wilmcote 99, 100
Wolston 32–5
Wood Norton 128, 129
Woollas Hall 144, 145
Workman Bridge 126
Wyre Piddle 132, 133

Shakespeare's Avon

WARWICKSHIRE

HEREFORD and WORCESTER

M 6

RYKNILD STREET

She

Hatton Rock

Was

Stratford-upon-Avon

Hampt Lucy

Wyre Piddle

Pershore

Salford Priors

Bidford-on-Avon

R. Arrow

Besford

Bow Brook

Abbot's Salford

Alveston

Wick

Fladbury

Harvington

R. Avon

Luddington

Defford

Chadbury

Charlecote Park

Pensham

Cropthorne

Charlton

Offenham

Marlcliff

Welford-on-Avon

Birlingham

Battlefield

Cleeve Hill

Cleeve Prior

Weston-on-Avon

Lower Strensham

Little Comberton

North Littleton

Eckington

Great Comberton

R. Stour

Upper Strensham

Middle Littleton

M 50

Elmley Castle

South Littleton

Twyning Green

Bredon's Norton

Bredon Hill

R. Isbourne

Evesham

Badsey Brook

BUCKLE STREET

R. Severn

R. Avon

Bredon

Overbury

Carrant Brook

R. Avon

Tewkesbury

Battlefield

M 6